Murder and black-market drugs were but part of Harry Lime's world—and now Rollo Martins was drawn into the picture. Would he be able to clear the name of his boyhood hero? Or would he work for the police to betray him?

"THE SINISTER EXCITEMENT OF DESPERATE ADVENTURES....

Mr. Greene builds up the suspense with loving care . . . has the insight to write about murder and espionage, flight and pursuit, as if they were horrible and abnormal activities. But the reason his stories pack the brutal wallop they do is Mr. Greene's conviction that such abnormalities are becoming commonplace in the modern world. By exaggerating this fundamental sense of outrage, Mr. Greene builds up a marvelously malevolent atmosphere. In a society beyond morality, Mr. Greene seems to suggest, murder is to be expected."
—*New York Herald Tribune*

THE THIRD MAN will ". . . succeed in scraping the nerves of even those who have seen the movie."
—*The New Yorker*

THE THIRD MAN
was originally published in the U.S. by The Viking Press.

Books by Graham Greene

Graham Greene

The
Third Man

PUBLISHED BY POCKET BOOKS NEW YORK

THE THIRD MAN

Trident edition published 1971

POCKET BOOK edition published September, 1974

Standard Book Number: 671-78393-9.
Library of Congress Catalog Card Number: 70-146055.
This POCKET BOOK edition is published by arrangement with the author's agent, International Famous Agency. Copyright, 1949, 1950, by Graham Greene. Copyright renewed, ©, 1964. All rights reserved. This book, or portions thereof, may not be reproduced by any means without permission of the author's agent: International Famous Agency, 1301 Avenue of the Americas, New York, N.Y. 10019.
Front cover illustration by Bob Berran.

Printed in the U.S.A.

To Carol Reed
in admiration and affection
and in memory of so many early morning
Vienna hours
at Maxim's, the Casanova, the Oriental

Preface

The Third Man was never written to be read but only to be seen. Like many love affairs it started at a dinner table and continued with many headaches in many places: Vienna, Venice, Ravello, London, Santa Monica.

Most novelists, I suppose, carry round in their heads or in their notebooks the first ideas for stories that have never come to be written. Sometimes one turns them over after many years and thinks regretfully that they would have been good once, in a time now dead. So, twenty years back, on the flap of an envelope, I had written an opening paragraph: "I had paid my last farewell to Harry a week ago, when his coffin was lowered into the frozen February ground, so that it was with incredulity that I saw him pass by, without a sign of recognition, among the host of strangers in the Strand." I, no more than my hero, had pursued Harry, so when Sir Alexander Korda asked me to write a film for Carol Reed—to follow our *Fallen Idol*—I had nothing more to offer than this paragraph. Though Korda wanted a film about the four-power occupation of Vienna, he was prepared to let me pursue the tracks of Harry Lime.

To me it is almost impossible to write a film play without first writing a story. Even a film depends on more than plot, on a certain measure of characterization, on mood and atmosphere; and these seem to me almost impossible to capture for the first time in the dull shorthand of a script. One can reproduce an effect caught in another medium, but one cannot make the first act of creation in script form. One must have the sense of more material than one needs to draw on. *The Third Man,* therefore, though never intended for publication, had to start as a story before it began those apparently interminable transformations from one treatment to another.

On these treatments Carol Reed and I worked closely together, covering so many feet of carpet a day, acting scenes at each other. No third ever joined our conferences; so much value lies in the clear cut-and-thrust of argument between two people. To the novelist, of course, his novel is the best he can do with a particular subject; he cannot help resenting many of the changes necessary for turning it into a film or a play; but *The Third Man* was never intended to be more than the raw material for a picture. The reader will notice many differences between the story and the film, and he should not imagine these changes were forced on an unwilling author: as likely as not they were suggested by the author. The film, in fact, is better than the story because it is in this case the finished state of the story.

Some of these changes have obvious superficial reasons. The choice of an American instead of an English star involved a number of alterations. For example, Mr. Joseph Cotten quite reasonably objected to the name Rollo. The name had to be an absurd one, and the name Holley occurred to me when I remembered that figure of fun, the American poet Thomas Holley Chivers. An American, too, could hardly have been mistaken for the great English writer Dexter, whose literary character bore certain echoes of the gentle genius of Mr. E. M. Forster. The confusion of identities would have been impossible, even if Carol Reed had not rightly objected to a rather far-fetched situation involving a great deal of explanation that increased the length of a film already far too long. Another minor point: in deference to American opinion a Rumanian was substituted for Cooler, since Mr. Orson Welles' engagement had already supplied us with one American villain. (Incidentally, the popular line of dialogue concerning Swiss cuckoo clocks was written into the script by Mr. Welles himself.)

One of the very few major disputes between Carol Reed and myself concerned the ending, and he has been proved triumphantly right. I held the view that an entertainment of this kind, which in England we call a thriller, was too light an affair to carry the weight of an unhappy ending. Reed on his side felt that my ending—indeterminate though it was, with no words spoken—would strike the audience, who had just seen Harry die, as unpleasantly cynical. I admit I was only half convinced; I was afraid few people would wait in their seats during the girl's long walk from the graveside and that they would leave the cinema under the impression that the ending was as conventional as mine and more drawn-out. I had not given enough consideration to the mastery of Reed's direction, and at that stage, of course, we neither of us could have anticipated Reed's brilliant discovery of Mr. Karas, the zither player.

The episode of the Russians kidnapping Anna (a perfectly possible incident in Vienna) was eliminated at a fairly late stage. It was not satisfactorily tied into the story, and it threatened to turn the film into a propagandist picture. We had no desire to move people's political emotions; we wanted to entertain them, to frighten them a little, to make them laugh.

Reality, in fact, was only a background to a fairy tale; nonetheless the story of the penicillin racket is based on a truth all the more grim because so many of the agents were more innocent than Joseph Harbin. The other day in London a surgeon took two friends to see the film. He was surprised to find them subdued and depressed by a picture he had enjoyed. They then told him that at the end of the war when they were with the Royal Air Force they had themselves sold penicillin in Vienna. The possible consequences of their act had never before occurred to them.

Boston, February 1950

The
Third Man

Story told largely by British police agent stationed in Vienna after end of World, but often in words of leading character Rollo Martins — what Martins told narrator after end of incident.

Plot is simple. Rollo Martins a British journalist, goes to Vienna at request of longtime friend, Harry Lime, on uncertain business. Martins arrives in V. only to find his friend dead. Suspecting foul play, he pursues matter by discovering + then visiting Lime's few friends at time of his death. So Martins visits Kurtz, Cooler, Anna Schmidt etc. He at last suspects that Lime is not dead + learns that Lime was in fact a leader of black market in penicillin, Lime killed someone else in his place to avert police. Martins discovers truth, + decides to betray his longtime friend to police. Lime eventually trapped in sewers of Vienna + killed.

Themes:
1) Education of innocent
2) Discovery of evil in guise of good
3) Process of disillusionment for Martins.

One

One never knows when the blow may fall. When I saw Rollo Martins first I made this note on him for my security police files: "In normal circumstances a cheerful fool. Drinks too much and may cause a little trouble. Whenever a woman passes raises his eyes and makes some comment, but I get the impression that really he'd rather not be bothered. Has never really grown up and perhaps that accounts for the way he worshipped Lime." I wrote there that phrase "in normal circumstances" because I met him first at Harry Lime's funeral. It was February, and the gravediggers had been forced to use electric drills to open the frozen ground in Vienna's Central Cemetery. It was as if even nature were doing its best to reject Lime, but we got him in at last and laid the earth back on him like bricks. He was vaulted in, and Rollo Martins walked quickly away as though his long gangly legs wanted to break into a run, and the tears of a boy ran down his thirty-five-year-old cheeks. Rollo Martins believed in friendship, and that was why what happened later was a worse shock to him than it would have been to you or me (you because you would have put it down to an illusion and me because at once a rational explanation—however wrongly—would have come to my mind). If only he had come to tell me then, what a lot of trouble would have been saved.

If you are to understand this strange rather sad story you must have an impression at least of the background—the smashed dreary city of Vienna divided up in zones among the four powers; the Russian, the British, the American, the French zones, regions marked only by notice boards, and in the centre of the city, surrounded by the Ring with its heavy public buildings and its prancing statuary, the Innere Stadt under the control of all four powers. In this once fashionable Innere Stadt each power in turn, for a month at a time, takes, as we call it, "the chair," and becomes responsible for security; at night, if you were fool enough to waste your Austrian schillings on a night club, you would be fairly certain to see the International Patrol at work—four military police, one from each power, communicating with each other, if they communicated at all, in the common language of their enemy. I never knew Vienna between the wars, and I am too young to remember the old Vienna with its Strauss music and its bogus easy charm; to me it is simply a city of undignified ruins which turned that February into great glaciers of snow and ice. The Danube was a grey flat muddy river a long way off across the second bezirk, the Russian zone, where the Prater lay smashed and desolate and full of weeds, only the Great Wheel revolving slowly over the foundations of merry-go-rounds like abandoned millstones, the rusting iron of smashed tanks which nobody had cleared away, the frost-nipped weeds where the snow was thin. I haven't enough imagination to picture it as it had once been, any more than I can picture Sacher's Hotel as other than a transit hotel for English officers or see the Kärntnerstrasse as a fashionable shopping street instead of a street which exists, most of it, only at eye level, repaired up to the first story. A Russian soldier in a fur cap goes by with a rifle over his shoulder, and men in overcoats sip ersatz coffee in the windows of the Old Vienna. This was roughly the Vienna to which Rollo Martins came on February seventh last year. I have reconstructed the affair as best I can from my own files and from what Martins told me. It is as accurate as I can make it—I haven't invented a line of dialogue, though I can't vouch for Martins' memory; an ugly story if you leave out the girl: grim and sad and unrelieved if it were not for that absurd episode of the British Cultural Relations Society lecturer.

Two

A British subject can still travel if he is content to take with him only five English pounds which he is forbidden to spend abroad, but if Rollo Martins had not received an invitation from Lime he would not have been allowed to enter Austria, which counts still as occupied territory. Lime had suggested that Martins might write up the business of looking after the international refugees, and although it wasn't Martins' usual line, he had consented. It would give him a holiday, and he badly needed a holiday after the incident in Dublin and the other incident in Amsterdam; he always tried to dismiss women as "incidents," things that simply happen to him without any will of his own, acts of God in the eyes of insurance agents. He had a haggard look when he arrived in Vienna and a habit of looking over his shoulder that for a time made me suspicious of him until I realized that he went in fear that one of, say, six people might turn up unexpectedly. He told me vaguely that he had been mixing his drinks —that was another way of putting it.

Rollo Martins' usual line was the writing of cheap paper-covered Westerns under the name of Buck Dexter. His public was large but unremunerative. He couldn't have afforded Vienna if Lime had not offered to pay his expenses when he got there out of some vaguely described propaganda fund. Lime could also, he said, keep him supplied with paper bafs—the only currency in use from a penny upwards in British hotels and clubs. So it was with exactly five unusable pound notes that Martins arrived in Vienna.

An odd incident had occurred at Frankfurt, where the plane from London grounded for an hour. Martins was eating a hamburger in the American canteen (a kindly airline supplied the passengers with a voucher for sixty-five cents' worth of food) when a man he could recognize from twenty feet away as a journalist approached his table.

"You Mr. Dexter?" he asked.

"Yes," Martins said, taken off his guard.

"You look younger than your photographs," the man said. "Like to make a statement? I represent the local forces paper here. We'd like to know what you think of Frankfurt."

"I only touched down ten minutes ago."

"Fair enough," the man said. "What about views on the American novel?"

"I don't read them," Martins said.

"The well-known acid humour," the journalist said. He pointed at a small grey-haired man with two protruding teeth, nibbling a bit of bread. "Happen to know if that's Carey?"

"No. What Carey?"

"J. G. Carey of course."

"I've never heard of him."

"You novelists live out of the world. He's my real assignment," and Martins watched him make across the room for the great Carey, who greeted him with a false headline smile, laying down his crust. Dexter wasn't the man's assignment, but Martins couldn't help feeling a certain pride—nobody had ever before referred to him as a novelist; and that sense of pride and importance carried him over the disappointment when Lime was not there to meet him at the airport. We never get accustomed to being less important to other people than they are to us—Martins felt the little jab of dispensability, standing by the bus door, watching the snow come sifting down, so thinly and softly that the great drifts among the ruined buildings had an air of permanence, as though they were not the result of this meagre fall, but lay, forever, above the line of perpetual snow.

There was no Lime to meet him at the Hotel Astoria where the bus landed him, and no message—only a cryptic one for Mr. Dexter from someone he had never heard of called Crabbin. "We expected you on tomorrow's plane. Please stay where you are. On the way round. Hotel room booked," but Rollo Martins wasn't the kind of man who stayed around. If you stayed around in a hotel lounge sooner or later incidents occurred; one mixed one's drinks. I can hear Rollo Martins saying to me now, "I've done with incidents. No more incidents," before he plunged head first into the most serious incident of all. There was always a conflict in Rollo Martins—between the absurd Christian name and the sturdy Dutch (four generations back) surname. Rollo looked at every woman that passed, and Martins renounced them forever. I don't know which of them wrote the Westerns.

Martins had been given Lime's address and he felt no curiosity about the man called Crabbin; it was too obvious that a mistake had been made, though he didn't yet connect it with the conversation at Frankfurt. Lime had written that he could put Martins up in his own

18

flat, a large apartment on the edge of Vienna that had been requisitioned from a Nazi owner. Lime could pay for the taxi when he arrived, so Martins drove straight away to the building lying in the third (British) zone. He kept the taxi waiting while he mounted to the third floor.

How quickly one becomes aware of silence even in so silent a city as Vienna with the snow steadily settling. Martins hadn't reached the second floor before he was convinced that he would not find Lime there, but the silence was deeper than just absence—it was as if he would not find Harry Lime anywhere in Vienna, and, as he reached the third floor and saw the big black bow over the door handle, anywhere in the world at all. Of course it might have been a cook who had died, a housekeeper, anybody but Harry Lime, but he knew —he felt he had known twenty stairs down—that Lime, the Lime he had hero-worshipped now for twenty years, since the first meeting in a grim school corridor with a cracked bell ringing for prayers, was gone. Martins wasn't wrong, not entirely wrong. After he had rung the bell half a dozen times a small man with a sullen expression put his head out from another flat and told him in a tone of vexation, "It's no use ringing like that. There's nobody there. He's dead."

"Herr Lime?"

"Herr Lime of course."

Martins said to me later, "At first it didn't mean a thing. It was just a bit of information, like those paragraphs in *The Times* they call 'News in Brief.' I said to him, 'When did it happen? How?' "

"He was run over by a car," the man said. "Last Thursday." He added sullenly, as if really this were none of his business, "They are burying him this afternoon. You've only just missed them."

"Them?"

"Oh, a couple of friends and the coffin."

"Wasn't he in hospital?"

"There was no sense in taking him to hospital. He was killed here on his own doorstep—instantaneously. The right-hand mud-guard struck him on his shoulder and bowled him over in front like a rabbit."

It was only then, Martins told me, when the man used the word "rabbit," that the dead Harry Lime came alive, became the boy with the gun which he had shown Martins the means of "borrowing"; a boy starting up among the long sandy barrows of Brickworth Common saying, "Shoot, you fool, shoot! There," and the rabbit limped to cover, wounded by Martins' shot.

"Where are they burying him?" he asked the stranger on the landing.

"In the Central Cemetery. They'll have a hard time of it in this frost."

He had no idea how to pay for his taxi, or indeed where in Vienna he could find a room in which he could live for five English pounds, but that problem had to be postponed until he had seen the last of Harry Lime. He drove straight out of town into the suburb (British zone) where the Central Cemetery lay. One passed through the Russian zone to reach it, and took a short cut through the American zone, which you couldn't mistake because of the ice-cream parlours in every street. The trams ran along the high wall of the Central Cemetery, and for a mile on the other side of the rails stretched the monumental masons and the market gardeners—an apparently endless chain of gravestones waiting for owners and wreaths waiting for mourners.

Martins had not realized the size of this huge snow-bound park where he was making his last rendezvous with Lime. It was as if Harry had left a message to him, "Meet me in Hyde Park," without specifying a spot between the Achilles statue and Lancaster Gate; the avenues of graves, each avenue numbered and lettered, stretched out like the spokes of an enormous wheel; they drove for a half-mile north, turned south. . . . The snow gave the great pompous family head-stones an air of grotesque comedy; a toupee of snow slipped sideways over an angelic face, a saint wore a heavy white moustache, and a shako of snow tipped at a drunken angle over the bust of a superior civil servant called Wolfgang Gottman. Even this cemetery was zoned between the powers: the Russian zone was marked by huge statues of armed men, the French by rows of anonymous wooden crosses and a torn tired tricolour flag. Then Martins remembered that Lime was a Catholic and was unlikely to be buried in the British one for which they had been vainly searching. So back they drove through the heart of a forest where the graves lay like wolves under the trees, winking white eyes under the gloom of the evergreens. Once from under the trees emerged a group of three men in strange eighteenth-century black and silver uniforms with three-cornered hats, pushing a kind of barrow: they crossed a ride in the forest of graves and disappeared again.

It was just chance that they found the funeral in time—one patch in the enormous park where the snow had been shovelled aside and a tiny group was gathered, apparently bent on some very private business. A priest was speaking, his words coming secretively through the thin patient snow, and a coffin was on the point of being lowered into the ground. Two men in lounge suits stood at the graveside; one carried a wreath that he obviously had forgotten to drop onto the coffin, for his companion nudged his elbow so that he came to with a start and dropped the flowers. A girl stood a little way away with her hands over her face, and I stood twenty yards away by another grave, watching with relief the last of Lime and noticing carefully who was there—just a man in a mackintosh I was to Martins. He came up to me and said, "Could you tell me who they are burying?"

"A fellow called Lime," I said, and was astonished to see the tears start to this stranger's eyes: he didn't look like a man who wept, nor was Lime the kind of man whom I thought likely to have mourners—genuine mourners with genuine tears. There was the girl of course, but one excepts women from all such generalizations.

Martins stood there, till the end, close beside me. He said to me later that as an old friend he didn't want to intrude on these newer ones—Lime's death belonged to them, let them have it. He was under the sentimental illusion that Lime's life—twenty years of it anyway—belonged to him. As soon as the affair was over—I am not a religious man and always feel a little impatient with the fuss that surrounds death—Martins strode away on his long gangly legs that always seemed likely to get entangled together, back to his taxi. He made no attempt to speak to anyone, and the tears now were really running, at any rate the few meagre drops that any of us can squeeze out at our age.

One's file, you know, is never quite complete; a case is never really closed, even after a century, when all the participants are dead. So I followed Martins: I knew the other three: I wanted to know the stranger. I caught him up by his taxi and said, "I haven't any transport. Would you give me a lift into town?"

"Of course," he said. I knew the driver of my jeep

would spot me as we came out and follow us unobtrusively. As we drove away I noticed he never looked behind—it's nearly always the fake mourners and the fake lovers who take that last look, who wait waving on platforms, instead of clearing quickly out, not looking back. Is it perhaps that they love themselves so much and want to keep themselves in the sight of others, even of the dead?

I said, "My name's Calloway."

"Martins," he said.

"You were a friend of Lime?"

"Yes." Most people in the last week would have hesitated before they admitted quite so much.

"Been here long?"

"I only came this afternoon from England. Harry had asked me to stay with him. I hadn't heard."

"Bit of a shock?"

"Look here," he said, "I badly want a drink, but I haven't any cash—except five pounds sterling. I'd be awfully grateful if you'd stand me one."

It was my turn to say "Of course." I thought for a moment and told the driver the name of a small bar in the Kärntnerstrasse. I didn't think he'd want to be seen for a while in a busy British bar full of transit officers and their wives. This bar—perhaps because it was exorbitant in its prices—seldom had more than one self-occupied couple in it at a time. The trouble was too that it really only had one drink—a sweet chocolate liqueur that the waiter improved at a price with cognac—but I got the impression that Martins had no objection to any drink so long as it cast a veil over the present, and the past. On the door was the usual notice saying the bar opened at six till ten, but one just pushed the door and walked through the front rooms. We had a whole small room to ourselves; the only couple were next door, and the waiter, who knew me, left us alone with some caviar sandwiches. It was lucky that we both knew that I had an expense account.

Martins said over his second quick drink, "I'm sorry, but he was the best friend I ever had."

I couldn't resist saying, knowing what I knew, and because I was anxious to vex him—one learns a lot that way—"That sounds like a cheap novelette."

He said quickly, "I write cheap novelettes."

I had learned something anyway. Until he had had a third drink I was under the impression that he wasn't an easy talker, but I felt fairly certain that he was one of those who turn unpleasant after their fourth glass.

I said, "Tell me about yourself—and Lime."

"Look here," he said, "I badly need another drink, but I can't keep on scrounging on a stranger. Could you change me a pound or two into Austrian money?"

"Don't bother about that," I said and called the waiter. "You can treat me when I come to London on leave. You were going to tell me how you met Lime?"

The glass of chocolate liqueur might have been a crystal, the way he looked at it and turned it this way and that. He said, "It was a long time ago. I don't suppose anyone knows Harry the way I do," and I thought of the thick file of agents' reports in my office, each claiming the same thing. I believe in my agents; I've sifted them all very thoroughly.

"How long?"

"Twenty years—or a bit more. I met him my first term at school. I can see the place. I can see the notice board and what was on it. I can hear the bell ringing. He was a year older and knew the ropes. He put me wise to a lot of things." He took a quick dab at his drink and then turned the crystal again as if to see more clearly what there was to see. He said, "It's funny. I can't remember meeting any woman quite as well."

"Was he clever at school?"

"Not the way they wanted him to be. But what things he did think up! He was a wonderful planner. I was far better at subjects like History and English than Harry, but I was a hopeless mug when it came to carrying out his plans." He laughed: he was already beginning, with the help of drink and talk, to throw off the shock of the death. He said, "I was always the one who got caught."

"That was convenient for Lime."

"What the hell do you mean?" he asked. Alcoholic irritation was setting in.

"Well, wasn't it?"

"That was my fault, not his. He could have found someone cleverer if he'd chosen, but he liked me. He was endlessly patient with me." Certainly, I thought, the child is father to the man, for I too had found him patient.

"When did you see him last?"

"Oh, he was over in London six months ago for a medical congress. You know he qualified as a doctor, though he never practised. That was typical of Harry. He just wanted to see if he could do a thing and then he lost interest. But he used to say that it often came in handy." And that too was true. It was odd how like the Lime he knew was to the Lime I knew: it was only that he looked at Lime's image from a different angle or in a different light. He said, "One of the things I liked about Harry was his humour." He gave a grin which took five years off his age. "I'm a buffoon, I like playing the silly fool, but Harry had real wit. You know, he could have been a first-class light composer if he had worked at it."

He whistled a tune—it was oddly familiar to me. "I always remember that. I saw Harry write it. Just in a couple of minutes on the back of an envelope. That was what he always whistled when he had something on his mind. It was his signature tune." He whistled the tune a second time, and I knew then who had written it—of course it wasn't Harry. I nearly told him so, but what was the point? The tune wavered and went out. He stared down into his glass, drained what was left, and said, "It's a damned shame to think of him dying the way he did."

"It was the best thing that ever happened to him," I said.

He didn't take in my meaning at once: he was a little hazy with the drinks. "The best thing?"

"Yes."

"You mean there wasn't any pain?"

"He was lucky in that way, too."

It was my tone of voice and not my words that caught Martins' attention. He asked gently and dangerously— I could see his right hand tighten—"Are you hinting at something?"

There is no point at all in showing physical courage in all situations: I eased my chair far enough back to be out of reach of his fists. I said, "I mean I had his case completed at police headquarters. He would have served a long spell—a very long spell—if it hadn't been for the accident."

"What for?"

"He was about the worst racketeer who ever made a dirty living in this city."

I could see him measuring the distance between us and deciding that he couldn't reach me from where he sat. Rollo wanted to hit out, but Martins was steady, careful. Martins, I began to realize, was dangerous. I wondered whether after all I had made a complete mistake: I couldn't see Martins being quite the mug that Rollo had made out. "You're a policeman?" he asked.

"Yes."

"I've always hated policemen. They are always either crooked or stupid."

"Is that the kind of books you write?"

I could see him edging his chair round to block my way out. I caught the waiter's eye and he knew what I meant—there's an advantage in always using the same bar for interviews.

Martins brought out a surface smile and said gently, "I have to call them sheriffs."

"Been in America?" It was a silly conversation.

"No. Is this an interrogation?"

"Just interest."

"Because if Harry was that kind of racketeer, I must be one too. We always worked together."

"I daresay he meant to cut you in—somewhere in the organization. I wouldn't be surprised if he had meant to give you the baby to hold. That was his method at school—you told me, didn't you? And, you see, the headmaster was getting to know a thing or two."

"You are running true to form, aren't you? I suppose there was some petty racket going on with petrol and you couldn't pin it on anyone, so you've picked a dead man. That's just like a policeman. You're a real policeman, I suppose?"

"Yes, Scotland Yard, but they've put me into a colonel's uniform when I'm on duty."

He was between me and the door now. I couldn't

27

get away from the table without coming into range, I'm no fighter, and he had six inches of advantage anyway. I said, "It wasn't petrol."

"Tires, saccharin—why don't you policemen catch a few murderers for a change?"

"Well, you could say that murder was part of his racket."

He pushed the table over with one hand and made a dive at me with the other; the drink confused his calculations. Before he could try again my driver had his arms round him. I said, "Don't treat him roughly. He's only a writer with too much drink in him."

"Be quiet, can't you, sir," my driver said. He had an exaggerated sense of officer-class. He would probably have called Lime "sir."

"Listen, Callaghan, or whatever your bloody name is . . ."

"Calloway. I'm English, not Irish."

"I'm going to make you look the biggest bloody fool in Vienna. There's one dead man you aren't going to pin your unsolved crimes on."

"I see. You're going to find me the real criminal? It sounds like one of your stories."

"You can let me go, Callaghan. I'd rather make you look the fool you are than black your bloody eye. You'd only have to go to bed for a few days with a black eye. But when I've finished with you you'll leave Vienna."

I took out a couple of pounds' worth of bafs and stuck them in his breast pocket. "These will see you through tonight," I said, "and I'll make sure they keep a seat for you on tomorrow's London plane."

"You can't turn me out. My papers are in order."

"Yes, but this is like other cities: you need money

here. If you change sterling on the black market I'll catch up on you inside twenty-four hours. Let him go."

Rollo Martins dusted himself down. He said, "Thanks for the drinks."

"That's all right."

"I'm glad I don't have to feel grateful. I suppose they were on expenses?"

"Yes."

"I'll be seeing you again in a week or two when I've got the dope." I knew he was angry; I didn't believe then that he was serious. I thought he was putting over an act to cheer up his self-esteem.

"I might come and see you off tomorrow."

"I shouldn't waste your time. I won't be there."

"Paine here will show you the way to Sacher's. You can get a bed and dinner there. I'll see to that."

He stepped to one side as though to make way for the waiter and slashed out at me. I just avoided him, but stumbled against the table. Before he could try again Paine had landed on him on the mouth. He went bang over in the alleyway between the tables and came up bleeding from a cut lip. I said, "I thought you promised not to fight."

He wiped some of the blood away with his sleeve and said, "Oh, no, I said I'd rather make you a bloody fool. I didn't say I wouldn't give you a black eye as well."

I had had a long day and I was tired of Rollo Martins. I said to Paine, "See him safely into Sacher's. Don't hit him again if he behaves," and, turning away from both of them towards the inner bar (I deserved one more drink), I heard Paine say respectfully to the man he had just knocked down, "This way, sir. It's only just around the corner."

Three

What happened next I didn't hear from Paine but from
Martins a long time afterwards, reconstructing the
chain of events that did indeed—though not quite in
the way he had expected—prove me to be a fool.
Paine simply saw him to the head porter's desk and
explained there, "This gentleman came in on the plane
from London. Colonel Calloway says he's to have a
room." Having made that clear, he said, "Good evening, sir," and left. He was probably a bit embarrassed
by Martins' bleeding lip.

"Had you already got a reservation, sir?" the porter
asked.

"No. No, I don't think so," Martins said in a muffled
voice holding his handkerchief to his mouth.

"I thought perhaps you might be Mr. Dexter. We
had a room reserved for a week for Mr. Dexter."

Martins said, "Oh, I am Mr. Dexter." He told me
later that it occurred to him that Lime might have
engaged him a room in that name because perhaps it
was Buck Dexter and not Rollo Martins who was to
be used for propaganda purposes. A voice said at his
elbow, "I'm so sorry you were not met at the plane,
Mr. Dexter. My name's Crabbin."

The speaker was a stout middle-aged man with a natural tonsure and one of the thickest pairs of horn-rimmed glasses that Martins had ever seen. He went apologetically on, "One of our chaps happened to ring up Frankfurt and heard you were on the plane. HQ made one of their usual foolish mistakes and wired you were not coming. Something about Sweden, but the cable was badly mutilated. Directly I heard from Frankfurt I tried to meet the plane, but I just missed you. You got my note?"

Martins held his handkerchief to his mouth and said obscurely, "Yes. Yes?"

"May I say at once, Mr. Dexter, how excited I am to meet you?"

"Good of you."

"Ever since I was a boy, I've thought you the greatest novelist of our century."

Martins winced. It was painful opening his mouth to protest. He took an angry look instead at Mr. Crabbin, but it was impossible to suspect that man of a practical joke.

"You have a big Austrian public, Mr. Dexter, both for your originals and your translations. Especially for *The Curved Prow,* that's my own favourite."

Martins was thinking hard. "Did you say—room for a week?"

"Yes."

"Very kind of you."

"Mr. Schmidt here will give you tickets every day, to cover all meals. But I expect you'll need a little pocket money. We'll fix that. Tomorrow we thought you'd like a quiet day—to look about."

"Yes."

"Of course any of us are at your service if you need a guide. Then the day after tomorrow in the evening

31

there's a little quiet discussion at the Institute—on the contemporary novel. We thought perhaps you'd say a few words just to set the ball rolling, and then answer questions."

Martins at that moment was prepared to agree to anything, to get rid of Mr. Crabbin and also to secure a week's free board and lodging; and Rollo, of course, as I was to discover later, had always been prepared to accept any suggestion—for a drink, for a girl, for a joke, for a new excitement. He said now, "Of course, of course," into his handkerchief.

"Excuse me, Mr. Dexter, have you got toothache? I know a very good dentist."

"No. Somebody hit me, that's all."

"Good God. Were they trying to rob you?"

"No, it was a soldier. I was trying to punch his bloody colonel in the eye." He removed the handkerchief and gave Crabbin a view of his cut mouth. He told me that Crabbin was at a complete loss for words. Martins couldn't understand why because he had never read the work of his great contemporary, Benjamin Dexter: he hadn't even heard of him. I am a great admirer of Dexter, so that I could understand Crabbin's bewilderment. Dexter has been ranked as a stylist with Henry James, but he has a wider feminine streak than his master—indeed his enemies have sometimes described his subtle, complex, wavering style as old-maidish. For a man still just on the right side of fifty his passionate interest in embroidery and his habit of calming a not very tumultuous mind with tatting—a trait beloved by his disciples—certainly to others seems a little affected.

"Have you ever read a book called *The Lone Rider of Santa Fe?*"

"No, I don't think so."

Martins said, "This lone rider had his best friend shot by the sheriff of a town called Lost Claim Gulch. The story is how he hunted that sheriff down—quite legally—until his revenge was completed."

"I never imagined you reading Westerns, Mr. Dexter," Crabbin said, and it needed all Martins' resolution to stop Rollo saying, "But I write them."

"Well, I'm gunning just the same way for Colonel Callaghan."

"Never heard of him."

"Heard of Harry Lime?"

"Yes," Crabbin said cautiously, "but I didn't really know him."

"I did. He was my best friend."

"I shouldn't have thought he was a very—literary character."

"None of my friends are."

Crabbin blinked nervously behind the horn-rims. He said with an air of appeasement, "He was interested in the theatre though. A friend of his—an actress, you know—is learning English at the Institute. He called once or twice to fetch her."

"Young or old?"

"Oh, young, very young. Not a good actress in my opinion."

Martins remembered the girl by the grave with her hands over her face. He said, "I'd like to meet any friend of Harry's."

"She'll probably be at your lecture."

"Austrian?"

"She claims to be Austrian, but I suspect she's Hungarian. She works at the Josefstadt. I wouldn't be surprised if Lime had helped her with her papers. She calls herself Schmidt. Anna Schmidt. You can't imagine a young English actress calling herself Smith, can you? And a pretty one, too. It always struck me as a bit too anonymous to be true."

Martins felt he had got all he could from Crabbin, so he pleaded tiredness, a long day, promised to ring up in the morning, accepted ten pounds' worth of bafs for immediate expenses, and went to his room. It seemed to him that he was earning money rapidly— twelve pounds in less than an hour.

He was tired: he realized that when he stretched himself out on his bed in his boots. Within a minute he had left Vienna far behind him and was walking through a dense wood, ankle deep in snow. An owl hooted, and he felt suddenly lonely and scared. He had an appointment to meet Harry under a particular tree, but in a wood so dense as this how could he recognize any one tree from the rest? Then he saw a figure and ran towards it; it whistled a familiar tune and his heart lifted with the relief and joy at not after all being alone. Then the figure turned and it was not Harry at all—just a stranger who grinned at him in a little circle of wet slushy melted snow, while the owl hooted again and again. He woke suddenly to hear the telephone ringing by his bed.

A voice with a trace of foreign accent—only a trace —said, "Is that Mr. Rollo Martins?"

"Yes." It was a change to be himself and not Dexter.

"You wouldn't know me," the voice said unnecessarily, "but I was a friend of Harry Lime."

It was a change too to hear anyone claim to be a friend of Harry's. Martins' heart warmed towards the stranger. He said, "I'd be glad to meet you."

"I'm just round the corner at the Old Vienna."

"Wouldn't you make it tomorrow? I've had a pretty awful day with one thing and another."

"Harry asked me to see that you were all right. I was with him when he died."

"I thought——" Rollo Martins said and stopped. He had been going to say "I thought he died instantaneously," but something suggested caution. He said instead, "You haven't told me your name."

"Kurtz," the voice said. "I'd offer to come round to you, only, you know, Austrians aren't allowed in Sacher's."

"Perhaps we could meet at the Old Vienna in the morning."

"Certainly," the voice said, "if you are *quite* sure that you are all right till then."

"How do you mean?"

"Harry had it on his mind that you'd be penniless." Rollo Martins lay back on his bed with the receiver to his ear and thought: Come to Vienna to make money. This was the third stranger to stake him in less than five hours. He said cautiously, "Oh, I can carry on till I see you." There seemed no point in turning down a good offer till he knew what the offer was.

"Shall we say eleven then at the Old Vienna in the Kärntnerstrasse? I'll be in a brown suit and I'll carry one of your books."

"That's fine. How did you get hold of one?"

"Harry gave it to me." The voice had enormous charm and reasonableness, but when Martins had said good night and rung off, he couldn't help wondering how it was that if Harry had been so conscious before he died he had not had a cable sent to stop him. Hadn't Callaghan too said that Lime had died instantaneously—or without pain, was it?—or had he himself put the words into Callaghan's mouth? It was then that the idea first lodged firmly in Martins' mind that there was something wrong about Lime's death, something the police had been too stupid to discover. He tried to discover it himself with the help of two cigarettes, but he fell asleep without his dinner and with the mystery still unsolved. It had been a long day, but not quite long enough for that.

Four

"What I disliked about him at first sight," Martins told me, "was his toupee. It was one of those obvious toupees—flat and yellow, with the hair cut straight at the back and not fitting close. There *must* be something phoney about a man who won't accept baldness gracefully. He had one of those faces too where the lines have been put in carefully, like a make-up, in the right places—to express charm, whimsicality, lines at the corners of the eyes. He was made up to appeal to romantic schoolgirls."

This conversation took place some days later—he brought out his whole story when the trail was nearly cold. When he made that remark about the romantic schoolgirls I saw his rather hunted eyes focus suddenly. It was a girl—just like any other girl, I thought —hurrying by outside my office in the driving snow.

"Something pretty?"

He brought his gaze back and said, "I'm off that forever. You know, Calloway, a time comes in a man's life when he gives up all that sort of thing . . ."

"I see. I thought you were looking at a girl."

"I was. But only because she reminded me for a moment of Anna—Anna Schmidt."

"Who's she? Isn't she a girl?"

"Oh, yes, in a way."

"What do you mean, in a way?"

"She was Harry's girl."

"Are you taking her over?"

"She's not that kind, Calloway. Didn't you see her at his funeral? I'm not mixing my drinks any more. I've got a hangover to last me a lifetime."

"You were telling me about Kurtz," I said.

It appeared that Kurtz was sitting there, making a great show of reading *The Lone Rider of Santa Fe*. When Martins sat down at his table he said with indescribably false enthusiasm, "It's wonderful how you keep the tension."

"Tension?"

"Suspense. You're a master at it. At the end of every chapter one's left guessing . . ."

"So you were a friend of Harry's," Martins said.

"I think his best," but Kurtz added with the smallest pause in which his brain must have registered the error, "except you of course."

"Tell me how he died."

"I was with him. We came out together from the door of his flat and Harry saw a friend he knew across the road—an American called Cooler. He waved to Cooler and started across the road to him when a jeep came tearing round the corner and bowled him over. It was Harry's fault really—not the driver's."

"Somebody told me he died instantaneously."

"I wish he had. He died before the ambulance could reach us though."

"He could speak then?"

"Yes. Even in his pain he worried about you."

"What did he say?"

"I can't remember the exact words, Rollo—I may

call you Rollo, mayn't I? he always called you that to us. He was anxious that I should look after you when you arrived. See that you were looked after. Get your return ticket for you." In telling me, Martins said, "You see I was collecting return tickets as well as cash."

"But why didn't you cable to stop me?"

"We did, but the cable must have missed you. What with censorship and the zones, cables can take anything up to five days."

"There was an inquest?"

"Of course."

"Did you know that the police have a crazy notion that Harry was mixed up in some racket?"

"No. But everyone in Vienna is. We all sell cigarettes and exchange schillings for bafs and that kind of thing."

"The police meant something worse than that."

"They get rather absurd ideas sometimes," the man with the toupee said cautiously.

"I'm going to stay here till I prove them wrong."

Kurtz turned his head sharply and the toupee shifted very very slightly. He said, "What's the good? Nothing can bring Harry back."

"I'm going to have that police officer run out of Vienna."

"I don't see what you can do."

"I'm going to start working back from his death. You were there and this man Cooler and the chauffeur. You can give me their addresses."

"I don't know the chauffeur's."

"I can get it from the coroner's records. And then there's Harry's girl . . ."

Kurtz said, "It will be painful for her."

"I'm not concerned about her. I'm concerned about Harry."

"Do you know what it is that the police suspect?"

"No. I lost my temper too soon."

"Has it occurred to you," Kurtz said gently, "that you might dig up something—well, discreditable to Harry?"

"I'll risk that."

"It will take a bit of time—and money."

"I've got time and you were going to lend me some money, weren't you?"

"I'm not a rich man," Kurtz said. "I promised Harry to see you were all right and that you got your plane back . . ."

"You needn't worry about the money—or the plane," Martins said. "But I'll make a bet with you—in pounds sterling—five pounds against two hundred schillings—that there's something queer about Harry's death."

It was a shot in the dark, but already he had this firm instinctive sense that there was something wrong, though he hadn't yet attached the word "murder" to the instinct. Kurtz had a cup of coffee halfway to his lips and Martins watched him. The shot apparently went wide; an unaffected hand held the cup to the mouth and Kurtz drank, a little noisily, in long sips. Then he put down the cup and said, "How do you mean— queer?"

"It was convenient for the police to have a corpse, but wouldn't it have been equally convenient, perhaps, for the real racketeers?" When he had spoken he realized that after all Kurtz had not been unaffected by his wild statement: hadn't he been frozen into caution and calm? The hands of the guilty don't necessarily tremble; only in stories does a dropped glass betray agitation. Tension is more often shown in the studied action. Kurtz had drunk his coffee as though nothing had been said.

"Well—" he took another sip—"of course I wish you luck, though I don't believe there's anything to find. Just ask me for any help you want."

"I want Cooler's address."

"Certainly. I'll write it down for you. Here it is. In the American zone."

"And yours?"

"I've already put it—underneath—in the Russian zone."

He rose, giving one of his studied Viennese smiles, the charm carefully painted in with a fine brush in the little lines about the mouth and eyes. "Keep in touch," he said, "and if you need help . . . but I still think you are very unwise." He touched *The Lone Rider*. "I'm so proud to have met you. A master of suspense," and one hand smoothed the toupee, while another, passing softly over the mouth, brushed out the smile as though it had never been.

Five

Martins sat on a hard chair just inside the stage door of the Josefstadt Theatre. He had sent up his card to Anna Schmidt after the matinée, marking it "a friend of Harry's." An arcade of little windows, with lace curtains and the lights going out one after another, showed where the artists were packing up for home, for the cup of coffee without sugar, the roll without butter to sustain them for the evening performance. It was like a little street built indoors for a film set, but even indoors it was cold, even cold to a man in a heavy overcoat, so that Martins rose and walked up and down, underneath the little windows. He felt, he said, a little like a Romeo who wasn't sure of Juliet's balcony.

He had had time to think: he was calm now, Martins not Rollo was in the ascendant. When a light went out in one of the windows and an actress descended into the passage where he walked, he didn't even turn to take a look. He was done with all that. He thought, Kurtz is right. They are all right. I'm behaving like a romantic fool. I'll just have a word with Anna Schmidt, a word of commiseration, and then I'll pack and go. He had quite forgotten, he told me, the complication of Mr. Crabbin.

A voice over his head called "Mr. Martins," and he looked up at the face that watched him from between the curtains a few feet above his head. It wasn't beautiful, he firmly explained to me, when I accused him of once again mixing his drinks. Just an honest face; dark hair and eyes which in that light looked brown; a wide forehead, a large mouth which didn't try to charm. No danger anywhere, it seemed to Rollo Martins, of that sudden reckless moment when the scent of hair or a hand against the side alters life. She said, "Will you come up, please? The second door on the right."

There are some people, he explained to me carefully, whom one recognizes instantaneously as friends. You can be at ease with them because you know that never, never will you be in danger. "That was Anna," he said, and I wasn't sure whether the past tense was deliberate or not.

Unlike most actresses' rooms this one was almost bare; no wardrobe packed with clothes, no clutter of cosmetics and grease paints: a dressing gown on the door, one sweater he recognized from Act II on the only easy chair, a tin of half-used paints and grease. A kettle hummed softly on a gas ring. She said, "Would you like a cup of tea? Someone sent me a packet last week—sometimes the Americans do, instead of flowers, you know, on the first night."

"I'd like a cup," he said, but if there was one thing he hated it was tea. He watched her while she made it, made it, of course, all wrong: the water not on the boil, the tea pot unheated, too few leaves. She said, "I never quite understand why English people like tea so."

He drank his cupful quickly like a medicine and watched her gingerly and delicately sip at hers. He said, "I wanted very much to see you. About Harry."

It was the dreadful moment; he could see her mouth stiffen to meet it.

"Yes?"

"I had known him twenty years. I was his friend. We were at school together, you know, and after that—there weren't many months running when we didn't meet . . ."

She said, "When I got your card, I couldn't say no. But there's nothing really for us to talk about, is there?—nothing."

"I wanted to hear—"

"He's dead. That's the end. Everything's over, finished. What's the good of talking?"

"We both loved him."

"I don't know. You can't know a thing like that— afterwards. I don't know anything any more except—"

"Except?"

"That I want to be dead too."

Martins told me, "Then I nearly went away. What was the good of tormenting her because of this wild idea of mine? But instead I asked her one question, 'Do you know a man called Cooler?' "

"An American?" she asked. "I think that was the man who brought me some money when Harry died. I didn't want to take it, but he said Harry had been anxious—at the last moment."

"So he didn't die instantaneously?"

"Oh, no."

Martins said to me, "I began to wonder why I had got that idea so firmly into my head, and then I thought it was only the man in the flat who told me so—no one else. I said to her, 'He must have been very clear in his head at the end—because he remembered about me too. That seems to show that there wasn't really any pain.' "

"That's what I tell myself all the time."

"Did you see the doctor?"

"Once. Harry sent me to him. He was Harry's own doctor. He lived nearby, you see."

Martins suddenly saw in that odd chamber of the mind that constructs such pictures, instantaneously, irrationally, a desert place, a body on the ground, a group of birds gathered. Perhaps it was a scene from one of his own books, not yet written, forming at the gate of consciousness. Immediately it faded, he thought how odd that they were all there, just at that moment, all Harry's friends—Kurtz, the doctor, this man Cooler; only the two people who loved him seemed to have been missing. He said, "And the driver? Did you hear his evidence?"

"He was upset, scared. But Cooler's evidençe exonerated him. No, it wasn't his fault, poor man. I've often heard Harry say what a careful driver he was."

"He knew Harry too?" Another bird flapped down and joined the others round the silent figure on the sand who lay face down. Now he could tell that it was Harry, by the clothes, by the attitude like that of a boy asleep in the grass at a playing field's edge, on a hot summer afternoon.

Somebody called outside the window, "Fraulein Schmidt."

She said, "They don't like one to stay too long. It uses up *their* electricity."

He had given up the idea of sparing her anything. He told her, "The police say they were going to arrest Harry. They'd pinned some racket on him."

She took the news in much the same way as Kurtz. "Everybody's in a racket."

"I don't believe he was in anything serious."

"No."

45

"But he may have been framed. Do you know a man called Kurtz?"

"I don't think so."

"He wears a toupee."

"Oh." He could tell that that struck home. He said, "Don't you think it was odd they were all there—at the death. Everybody knew Harry. Even the driver, the doctor . . ."

She said with hopeless calm, "I've thought that too, though I didn't know about Kurtz. I wondered whether they'd murdered him, but what's the use of wondering?"

"I'm going to get those bastards," Rollo Martins said.

"It won't do any good. Perhaps the police are right. Perhaps poor Harry got mixed up—"

"Fraulein Schmidt," the voice called again.

"I must go."

"I'll walk with you a bit of the way."

The dark was almost down; the snow had ceased for a while to fall, and the great statues of the Ring, the prancing horses, the chariots and the eagles, were gunshot grey with the end of evening light. "It's better to give up and forget," Anna said. The moony snow lay ankle deep on the unswept pavements.

"Will you give me the doctor's address?"

They stood in the shelter of a wall while she wrote it down for him.

"And yours too?"

"Why do you want that?"

"I might have news for you."

"There isn't any news that would do any good now." He watched her from a distance board her tram, bowing her head against the wind, a little dark question mark on the snow.

Six

An amateur detective has this advantage over the professional, that he doesn't work set hours. Rollo Martins was not confined to the eight-hour day: his investigations didn't have to pause for meals. In this one day he covered as much ground as one of my men would have covered in two, and he had this initial advantage over us, that he was Harry's friend. He was, as it were, working from inside, while we pecked at the perimeter.

Dr. Winkler was at home. Perhaps he would not have been at home to a police officer. Again Martins had marked his card with the sesame phrase: "A friend of Harry Lime's."

Dr. Winkler's waiting room reminded Martins of an antique shop—an antique shop that specialized in religious objets d'art. There were more crucifixes than he could count, none of later date probably than the seventeenth century. There were statues in wood and ivory. There were a number of reliquaries: little bits of bone marked with saints' names and set in oval frames on a background of tinfoil. If they were genuine, what an odd fate it was, Martins thought, for a portion of Saint Susanna's knuckle to come to rest in Dr. Winkler's waiting room. Even the high-backed hideous chairs looked as if they had once been sat in by cardinals. The room was stuffy, and one expected the smell of incense. In a small gold casket was a splinter of the True Cross. A sneeze disturbed him.

Dr. Winkler was the cleanest doctor Martins had ever seen. He was very small and neat, in a black tail coat and a high stiff collar; his little black moustache was like an evening tie. He sneezed again: perhaps he was cold because he was so clean. He said, "Mr. Martins?"

An irresistible desire to sully Dr. Winkler assailed Rollo Martins. He said, "Dr. Winkle?"

"Dr. Winkler."

"You've got an interesting collection here."

"Yes."

"These saints' bones . . ."

"The bones of chickens and rabbits." Dr. Winkler took a large white handkerchief out of his sleeve rather as though he were a conjurer producing his country's flag, and blew his nose neatly and thoroughly twice, closing each nostril in turn. You expected him to throw away the handkerchief after one use. "Would you mind, Mr. Martins, telling me the purpose of your visit? I have a patient waiting."

"We were both friends of Harry Lime."

"I was his medical adviser," Dr. Winkler corrected him and waited obstinately between the crucifixes.

"I arrived too late for the inquest. Harry had invited me out here to help him in something. I don't quite know what. I didn't hear of his death till I arrived."

"Very sad," Dr. Winkler said.

"Naturally, under the circumstances, I want to hear all I can."

"There is nothing I can tell you that you don't

48

know. He was knocked over by a car. He was dead when I arrived."

"Would he have been conscious at all?"

"I understand he was for a short time, while they carried him into the house."

"In great pain?"

"Not necessarily."

"You are quite certain that it was an accident?"

Dr. Winkler put out a hand and straightened a crucifix. "I was not there. My opinion is limited to the cause of death. Have you any reason to be dissatisfied?"

The amateur has another advantage over the professional: he can be reckless. He can tell unnecessary truths and propound wild theories. Martins said, "The police had implicated Harry in a very serious racket. It seemed to me that he might have been murdered—or even killed himself."

"I am not competent to pass an opinion," Dr. Winkler said.

"Do you know a man called Cooler?"

"I don't think so."

"He was there when Harry was killed."

"Then of course I have met him. He wears a toupee."

"That was Kurtz."

Dr. Winkler was not only the cleanest, he was also the most cautious doctor that Martins had ever met. His statements were so limited that you could not for a moment doubt their veracity. He said, "There was a second man there." If he had to diagnose a case of scarlet fever he would, you felt, have confined himself to a statement that a rash was visible, that the temperature was so and so. He would never find himself in error at an inquest.

"Had you been Harry's doctor for long?" He seemed

an odd man for Harry to choose—Harry who liked men with a certain recklessness, men capable of making mistakes.

"For about a year."

"Well, it's good of you to have seen me." Dr. Winkler bowed. When he bowed there was a very slight creak as though his shirt were made of celluloid. "I mustn't keep you from your patients any longer." Turning away from Dr. Winkler, he confronted yet another crucifix, the figure hanging with arms above the head: a face of elongated El Greco agony. "That's a strange crucifix," he said.

"Jansenist," Dr. Winkler commented and closed his mouth sharply as though he had been guilty of giving away too much information.

"Never heard the word. Why are the arms above the head?"

Dr. Winkler said reluctantly, "Because He died, in their view, only for the elect."

Seven

As I see it, turning over my files, the notes of conversations, the statements of various characters, it would have been still possible, at this moment, for Rollo Martins to have left Vienna safely. He had shown an unhealthy curiosity, but the disease had been checked at every point. Nobody had given anything away. The smooth wall of deception had as yet shown no real crack to his roaming fingers. When Rollo Martins left Dr. Winkler's he was in no danger. He could have gone home to bed at Sacher's and slept with a quiet mind. He could even have visited Cooler at this stage without trouble. No one was seriously disturbed. Unfortunately for him—and there would always be periods of his life when he bitterly regretted it—he chose to go back to Harry's flat. He wanted to talk to the little vexed man who said he had seen the accident—or had he really not said so much? There was a moment in the dark frozen street when he was inclined to go straight to Cooler, to complete his picture of those sinister birds who sat around Harry's body, but Rollo, being Rollo, decided to toss a coin and the coin fell for the other action, and the deaths of two men.

Perhaps the little man—who bore the name of Koch—had drunk a glass too much of wine, perhaps he had simply spent a good day at the office, but this time, when Rollo Martins rang his bell, he was friendly and quite ready to talk. He had just finished dinner and had crumbs on his moustache. "Ah, I remember you. You are Herr Lime's friend."

He welcomed Martins in with great cordiality and introduced him to a mountainous wife whom he obviously kept under very strict control. "Ah, in the old days I would have offered you a cup of coffee, but now—"

Martins passed round his cigarette case and the atmosphere of cordiality deepened. "When you rang yesterday I was a little abrupt," Herr Koch said, "but I had a touch of migraine and my wife was out, so I had to answer the door myself."

"Did you tell me that you had actually seen the accident?"

Herr Koch exchanged glances with his wife. "The inquest is over, Ilse. There is no harm. You can trust my judgment. The gentleman is a friend. Yes, I saw the accident, but you are the only one who knows. When I say that I saw it, perhaps I should say that I heard it. I heard the brakes put on and the sound of the skid, and I got to the window in time to see them carry the body to the house."

"But didn't you give evidence?

"It is better not to be mixed up in such things. My office cannot spare me. We are short of staff, and of course I did not actually see—"

"But you told me yesterday how it happened."

"That was how they described it in the papers."

"Was he in great pain?"

"He was dead. I looked right down from my window here and I saw his face. I know when a man is dead. You see, it is, in a way, my business. I am the head clerk at the mortuary."

"But the others say that he did not die at once."

"Perhaps they don't know death as well as I do."

"He was dead, of course, when the doctor arrived. He told me that."

"He was dead at once. You can take the word of a man who knows."

"I think, Herr Koch, that you should have given evidence."

"One must look after oneself, Herr Martins. I was not the only one who should have been there."

"How do you mean?"

"There were three people who helped to carry your friend to the house."

"I know—two men and the driver."

"The driver stayed where he was. He was very much shaken, poor man."

"Three men . . ." It was as though suddenly, fingering that bare wall, his fingers had encountered not so much a crack perhaps but at least a roughness that had not been smoothed away by the careful builders.

"Can you describe the men?"

But Herr Koch was not trained to observe the living: only the man with the toupee had attracted his eyes—the other two were just men, neither tall nor short, thick nor thin. He had seen them from far above, foreshortened, bent over their burden; they had not looked up, and he had quickly looked away and closed the window, realizing at once the wisdom of not being seen himself.

"There was no evidence I could really give, Herr Martins."

53

No evidence, Martins thought, no evidence! He no longer doubted that murder had been done. Why else had they lied about the moment of death? They wanted to quiet with their gifts of money and their plane ticket the only two friends Harry had in Vienna. And the third man? Who was he?

He said, "Did you see Herr Lime go out?"

"No."

"Did you hear a scream?"

"Only the brakes, Herr Martins."

It occured to Martins that there was nothing—except the word of Kurtz and Cooler and the driver—to prove that in fact Harry had been killed at that precise moment. There was the medical evidence, but that could not prove more than that he had died, say, within a half-hour, and in any case the medical evidence was only as strong as Dr. Winkler's word: that clean controlled man creaking among his crucifixes.

"Herr Martins, it just occurs to me—you are staying in Vienna?"

"Yes."

"If you need accommodation and spoke to the authorities quickly, you might secure Herr Lime's flat. It is a requisitioned property."

"Who has the keys?"

"I have them."

"Could I see the flat?"

"Ilse, the keys."

Herr Koch led the way into the flat that had been Harry's. In the little dark hall there was still the smell of cigarette smoke—the Turkish cigarettes that Harry always smoked. It seemed odd that a man's smell should cling in the folds of curtains so long after the man himself had become dead matter, a gas, a decay.

One light, in a heavily beaded shade, left them in semi-darkness, fumbling for door handles.

The living room was completely bare—it seemed to Martins too bare. The chairs had been pushed up against the walls; the desk at which Harry must have written was free from dust or any papers. The parquet reflected the light like a mirror. Herr Koch opened a door and showed the bedroom: the bed neatly made with clean sheets. In the bathroom not even a used razor blade indicated that a few days ago a living man had occupied it. Only the dark hall and the cigarette smell gave a sense of occupation.

"You see," Herr Koch said, "it is quite ready for a newcomer. Ilse has cleaned up."

That she certainly had done. After a death there should have been more litter left than this. A man can't go suddenly and unexpectedly on his longest journey without forgetting this or that, without leaving a bill unpaid, an official form unanswered, the photograph of a girl. "Were there no papers, Herr Koch?"

"Herr Lime was always a very tidy man. His waste-paper basket was full and his brief case, but his friend fetched that way."

His friend?"

"The gentleman with the toupee."

It was possible, of course, that Lime had not taken the journey so unexpectedly, and it occurred to Martins that Lime had perhaps hoped he would arrive in time to help. He said to Herr Koch, "I believe my friend was murdered."

"Murdered?" Herr Koch's cordiality was snuffed out by the word. He said, "I would not have asked you in here if I had thought you would talk such nonsense."

"All the same your evidence may be very valuable."

"I have no evidence. I saw nothing. I am not concerned. You must leave here at once please. You have been very inconsiderate." He hustled Martins back through the hall; already the smell of the smoke was fading a little more. Herr Koch's last word before he slammed his own door was, "It's no concern of mine." Poor Herr Koch! We do not choose our concerns. Later, when I was questioning Martins closely, I said to him, "Did you see anybody at all on the stairs, or in the street outside?"

"Nobody." He had everything to gain by remembering some chance passer-by, and I believed him. He said, "I noticed myself how quiet and dead the whole street looked. Part of it had been bombed, you know, and the moon was shining on the snow slopes. It was so very silent. I could hear my own feet creaking in the snow."

"Of course it proves nothing. There is a basement where anybody who had followed you could have hidden."

"Yes."

"Or your whole story may be phoney."

"Yes."

"The trouble is I can see no motive for you to have done it. It's true you are already guilty of getting money on false pretences. You came out here to join Lime, perhaps to help him . . ."

Martins said to me, "What was this precious racket you keep on hinting at?"

"I'd have told you all the facts when I first saw you if you hadn't lost your temper so damned quickly. Now I don't think I shall be acting wisely to tell you. It would be disclosing official information, and your contacts, you know, don't inspire confidence. A girl with phoney papers supplied by Lime, this man Kurtz . . ."

"Dr. Winkler . . ."

"I've got nothing against Dr. Winkler. No, if you are phoney, you don't need the information, but it might help you to learn exactly what we know. You see, our facts are not complete."

"I bet they aren't. I could invent a better detective than you in my bath."

"Your literary style does not do your namesake justice." Whenever he was reminded of Mr. Crabbin, that poor harassed representative of the British Cultural Relations Society, Rollo Martins turned pink with annoyance, embarrassment, shame. That too inclined me to trust him.

He had certainly given Crabbin some uncomfortable hours. On returning to Sacher's Hotel after his interview with Herr Koch he had found a desperate note waiting for him from the representative.

"I have been trying to locate you all day," Crabbin wrote. "It is essential that we should get together and work out a proper programme for you. This morning by telephone I have arranged lectures at Innsbruck and Salzburg for next week, but I must have your consent to the subjects, so that proper programmes can be printed. I would suggest two lectures: 'The Crisis of Faith in the Western World' (you are very respected here as a Christian writer, but this lecture should be quite unpolitical) and 'The Technique of the Contemporary Novel.' The same lectures would be given in Vienna. Apart from this, there are a great many people here who would like to meet you, and I want to arrange a cocktail party for early next week. But for all this I must have a few words with you." The letter ended on a note of acute anxiety. "You will be at the discussion tomorrow night, won't you? We all expect you at 8:30 and, needless to say, look forward to your coming. I will send transport to the hotel at 8:15 sharp."

Rollo Martins read the letter and, without bothering any further about Mr. Crabbin, went to bed.

Eight

After two drinks Rollo Martins' mind would always turn towards women—in a vague, sentimental, romantic way, as a sex, in general. After three drinks, like a pilot who dives to find direction, he would begin to focus on one available girl. If he had not been offered a third drink by Cooler, he would probably not have gone quite so soon to Anna Schmidt's house, and if— but there are too many "ifs" in my style of writing, for it is my profession to balance possibilities, human possibilities, and the drive of destiny can never find a place in my files.

Martins had spent his lunchtime reading up the reports of the inquest, thus again demonstrating the superiority of the amateur to the professional, and making him more vulnerable to Cooler's liquor (which the professional in duty bound would have refused). It was nearly five o'clock when he reached Cooler's flat, which was over an ice-cream parlour in the American zone: the bar below was full of G.I.'s with their girls, and the clatter of the long spoons and the curious free uniformed laughter followed him up the stairs.

The Englishman who objects to Americans in general usually carries in his mind's eye just such an exception as Cooler: a man with tousled grey hair and a worried kindly face and long-sighted eyes, the kind of humanitarian who turns up in a typhus epidemic or a world war or a Chinese famine long before his countrymen have discovered the place in an atlas. Again the card marked "Harry's friend" was like an entrance ticket. The warm frank handclasp was the most friendly act that Martins had encountered in Vienna.

"Any friend of Harry is all right with me," Cooler said. "I've heard of you, of course."

"From Harry?"

"I'm a great reader of Westerns," Cooler said, and Martins believed him as he did not believe Kurtz.

"I wondered—you were there, weren't you?—if you'd tell me about Harry's death."

"It was a terrible thing," Cooler said. "I was just crossing the road to go to Harry. He and Mr. Kurtz were on the sidewalk. Maybe if I hadn't started across the road, he'd have stayed where he was. But he saw me and stepped straight off to meet me and this jeep—it was terrible, terrible. The driver braked, but he didn't stand a chance. Have a Scotch, Mr. Martins. It's silly of me, but I get shaken up when I think of it." He said as he splashed in the soda, "I'd never seen a man killed before."

"Was the other man in the car?"

Cooler took a long pull and then measured what was left with his tired kindly eyes. "What man would you be referring to, Mr. Martins?"

"I was told there was another man there."

"I don't know how you got that idea. You'll find all about it in the inquest reports." He poured out two more generous drinks. "There were just the three of us—me and Mr. Kurtz and the driver. The doctor, of course. I expect you were thinking of the doctor."

"This man I was talking to happened to look out of a window—he has the next flat to Harry's—and he said he saw three men and the driver. That's before the doctor arrived."

"He didn't say that in court."

"He didn't want to get involved."

"You'll never teach these Europeans to be good citizens. It was his duty." Cooler brooded sadly over his glass. "It's an odd thing, Mr. Martins, with accidents. You'll never get two reports that coincide. Why, even I and Mr. Kurtz disagreed about details. The thing happens so suddenly you aren't concerned to notice things, until bang crash, and then you have to reconstruct, remember. I expect he got too tangled up trying to sort out what happened before and what after, to distinguish the four of us."

"The four?"

"I was counting Harry. What else did he see, Mr. Martins?"

"Nothing of interest—except he says Harry was dead when he was carried to the house."

"Well, he was dying—not much difference there. Have another drink, Mr. Martins?"

"No, I don't think I will."

"Well, I'd like another spot. I was very fond of your friend, Mr. Martins, and I don't like talking about it."

"Perhaps one more—to keep you company."

"Do you know Anna Schmidt?" Martins asked, while the whisky still tingled on his tongue.

"Harry's girl? I met her once, that's all. As a matter of fact, I helped Harry fix her papers. Not the sort of thing I should confess to a stranger, I suppose, but you have to break the rules sometimes. Humanity's a duty too."

"What was wrong?"

"She was Hungarian and her father had been a Nazi, so they said. She was scared the Russians would pick her up."

"Why should they want to?"

"Well, her papers weren't in order."

"You took her some money from Harry, didn't you?"

"Yes, but I wouldn't have mentioned that. Did she tell you?"

The telephone rang, and Cooler drained his glass. "Hullo," he said. "Why, yes. This is Cooler." Then he sat with the receiver at his ear and an expression of sad patience, while some voice a long way off drained into the room. "Yes," he said once. "Yes." His eyes dwelt on Martins' face, but they seemed to be looking a long way beyond him: flat and tired and kind, they might have been gazing out across the sea. He said, "You did quite right," in a tone of commendation, and then, with a touch of asperity, "Of course they will be delivered. I gave my word. Good-bye."

He put the receiver down and passed a hand across his forehead wearily. It was as though he were trying to remember something he had to do. Martins said, "Had you heard anything of this racket the police talk about?"

"I'm sorry. What's that?"

"They say Harry was mixed up in some racket."

"Oh, no," Cooler said. "No. That's quite impossible. He had a great sense of duty."

"Kurtz seemed to think it was possible."

"Kurtz doesn't understand how an Anglo-Saxon feels," Cooler replied.

Nine

It was nearly dark when Martins made his way along the banks of the canal: across the water lay the half-destroyed Diana baths and in the distance the great black circle of the Prater Wheel, stationary above the ruined houses. Over there across the grey water was the second bezirk, in Russian ownership. St. Stefanskirche shot its enormous wounded spire into the sky above the Inner City, and, coming up the Kärntnerstrasse, Martins passed the lit door of the Military Police station. The four men of the International Patrol were climbing into their jeep; the Russian M.P. sat beside the driver (for the Russians had that day taken over the chair for the next four weeks) and the Englishman, the Frenchman, and the American mounted behind. The third stiff whisky fumed into Martins' brain, and he remembered the girl in Amsterdam, the girl in Paris; loneliness moved along the crowded pavement at his side. He passed the corner of the street where Sacher's lay and went on. Rollo was in control and moved towards the only girl he knew in Vienna.

I asked him how he knew where she lived. Oh, he said, he'd looked up the address she had given him the night before, in bed, studying a map. He wanted to know his way about, and he was good with maps. He could memorize turnings and street names easily because he always went one way on foot.

"One way?"

"I mean when I'm calling on a girl—or someone."

He hadn't, of course, known that she would be in, that her play was not on that night in the Josefstadt, or perhaps he had memorized that too from the posters. In at any rate she was, if you could really call it being in, sitting alone in an unheated room, with the bed disguised as a divan, and a typewritten script lying open at the first page on the inadequate too-fancy topply table—because her thoughts were so far from being "in." He said awkwardly (and nobody could have said, not even Rollo, how much his awkwardness was part of his technique), "I thought I'd just look in and look you up. You see I was passing . . ."

"Passing? Where to?" It had been a good half an hour's walk from the Inner City to the rim of the English zone, but he always had a reply. "I had too much whisky with Cooler. I needed a walk and I just happened to find myself this way."

"I can't give you a drink here. Except tea. There's some of that packet left."

"No, no thank you." He said, "You are busy," looking at the script.

"I didn't get beyond the first line."

He picked it up and read: *"Enter Louise.* LOUISE: I heard a child crying."

"Can I stay a little?" he asked with a gentleness that was more Martins than Rollo.

"I wish you would." He slumped down on the divan, and he told me a long time later (for lovers talk and reconstruct the smallest details if they can find a listener) that there it was he took his second real look at her. She stood there as awkward as himself in a pair of old flannel trousers which had been patched badly in the seat; she stood with her legs firmly straddled as though she were opposing someone and was determined to hold her ground—a small rather stocky figure with any grace she had folded and put away for use professionally.

"One of those bad days?" he asked.

"It's always bad about this tme." She explained, "He used to look in, and when I heard your ring, just for a moment, I thought . . ." She sat down on a hard chair opposite him and said, "Please talk. You knew him. Just tell me anything."

And so he talked. The sky blackened outside the window while he talked. He noticed after a while that their hands had met. He said to me, "I never meant to fall in love, not with Harry's girl."

"When did it happen?" I asked him.

"It was very cold and I got up to close the window curtains. I only noticed my hand was on hers when I took it away. As I stood up I looked down at her face and she was looking up. It wasn't a beautiful face—that was the trouble. It was a face to live with, day in, day out. A face for wear. I felt as though I'd come into a new country where I couldn't speak the language. I had always thought it was beauty one loved in a woman. I stood there at the curtains, waiting to pull them, looking out. I couldn't see anything but my own face, looking back into the room, looking for her. She said, 'And what did Harry do that time?' and I wanted to say, 'Damn Harry. He's dead. We both loved him, but he's dead. The dead are made to be forgotten.' Instead of course all I said was, 'What do you think? He just whistled his old tune as if nothing was the matter,' and I whistled it to her as well as I could.

I heard her catch her breath, and I looked round and before I could think, is this the right way, the right card, the right gambit?—I'd already said, 'He's dead. You can't go on remembering him forever.' "

She said, "I know, but perhaps something will happen first."

"What do you mean—something happen?"

"Oh, I mean, perhaps there'll be another way, or I'll die, or something."

"You'll forget him in time. You'll fall in love again."

"I know, but I don't want to. Don't you see I don't want to."

So Rollo Martins came back from the window and sat down on the divan again. When he had risen half a minute before he had been the friend of Harry, comforting Harry's girl; now he was a man in love with Anna Schmidt who had been in love with a man they had both once known called Harry Lime. He didn't speak again that evening about the past. Instead he began to tell her of the people he had seen. "I can believe anything of Winkler," he told her, "but Cooler —I liked Cooler. He was the only one of his friends who stood up for Harry. The trouble is, if Cooler's right, then Koch is wrong, and I really thought I had something there."

"Who's Koch?"

He explained how he had returned to Harry's flat and he described his interview with Koch, the story of the third man.

"If it's true," she said, "it's very important."

"It doesn't prove anything. After all, Koch backed out of the inquest; so might this stranger."

"That's not the point," she said. "It means that *they* lied. Kurtz and Cooler."

"They might have lied so as not to inconvenience this fellow—if he was a friend."

"Yet another friend—on the spot. And where's your Cooler's honesty then?"

"What do we do? He clamped down like an oyster and turned me out of his flat."

"He won't turn me out," she said, "or his Ilse won't."

They walked up the long road to the flat together; the snow clogged on their shoes and made them move slowly like convicts weighed down by irons. Anna Schmidt said, "Is it far?"

"Not very far now. Do you see that knot of people up the road? It's somewhere about there." The group of people up the road was like a splash of ink on the whiteness that flowed, changed shape, spread out. When they came a little nearer Martins said, "I think that is his block. What do you suppose this is, a political demonstration?"

Anna Schmidt stopped. She said, "Who else have you told about Koch?"

"Only you and Cooler. Why?

"I'm frightened. It reminds me . . ." She had her eyes fixed on the crowd and he never knew what memory out of her confused past had risen to warn her. "Let's go away," she implored him.

"You're crazy. We're on to something here, something big . . ."

"I'll wait for you."

"But you're going to talk to him."

"Find out first what all those people . . ." She said strangely for one who worked behind the footlights, "I hate crowds."

He walked slowly on alone, the snow caking on his heels. It wasn't a political meeting, for no one was making a speech. He had the impression of heads turning to watch him come, as though he were somebody who was expected. When he reached the fringe of the little crowd, he knew for certain that it was the house. A man looked hard at him and said, "Are you another of them?"

"What do you mean?"

"The police."

"No. What are they doing?"

"They've been in and out all day."

"What's everybody waiting for?"

"They want to see him brought out."

"Who?"

"Herr Koch." It occurred vaguely to Martins that somebody besides himself had discovered Herr Koch's failure to give evidence, though that was hardly a police matter. He said, "What's he done?"

"Nobody knows that yet. They can't make their minds up in there—it might be suicide, you see, and it might be murder."

"Herr Koch?"

"Of course."

A small child came up to his informant and pulled at his hand. "Papa, Papa." He wore a wool cap on his head, like a gnome; his face was pinched and blue with cold.

"Yes, my dear, what is it?"

"I heard them talking through the grating, Papa."

"Oh, you cunning little one. Tell us what you heard, Hansel."

"I heard Frau Koch crying, Papa."

"Was that all, Hansel?"

"No. I heard the big man talking, Papa."

"Ah, you cunning little Hansel. Tell Papa what he said."

"He said, 'Can you tell me, Frau Koch, what the foreigner looked like?' "

"Ha, ha, you see, they think it's murder. And who's to say they are wrong? Why should Herr Koch cut his own throat in the basement?"

"Papa, Papa."

"Yes, little Hansel?"

"When I looked through the grating, I could see some blood on the coke."

"What a child you are. How could you tell it was blood? The snow leaks everywhere." The man turned to Martins and said, "The child has such an imagination. Maybe he will be a writer when he grows up."

The pinched face stared solemnly up at Martins. The child said, "Papa."

"Yes, Hansel?"

"He's a foreigner too."

The man gave a big laugh that caused a dozen heads to turn. "Listen to him, sir, listen," he said proudly. "He thinks you did it just because you are a foreigner. As though there weren't more foreigners here these days than Viennese."

"Papa, Papa."

"Yes, Hansel?"

"They are coming out."

A knot of police surrounded the covered stretcher which they lowered carefully down the steps for fear of sliding on the trodden snow. The man said, "They can't get an ambulance into this street because of the ruins. They have to carry it round the corner." Frau Koch came out at the tail of the procession; she had a shawl over her head and an old sackcloth coat. Her thick shape looked like a snowman as she sank in a drift at the pavement's edge. Someone gave her a hand and she looked round with a lost hopeless gaze at this crowd of strangers. If there were friends there she did not recognize them, looking from face to face. Martins bent as she passed, fumbling at his shoelace, but looking up from the ground he saw at his own eyes' level the scrutinizing cold-blooded gnome gaze of little Hansel.

Walking back down the street towards Anna, he looked back once. The child was pulling at his father's hand and he could see the lips forming round those syllables like the refrain of a grim bailad, "Papa, Papa."

He said to Anna, "Koch has been murdered. Come away from here." He walked as rapidly as the snow would let him, turning this corner and that. The child's suspicion and alertness seemed to spread like a cloud over the city—they could not walk fast enough to evade its shadow. He paid no attention when Anna said to him, "Then what Koch said was true. There *was* a third man," nor a little later when she said, "It must have been murder. You don't kill a man to hide anything less."

The tramcars flashed like icicles at the end of the street: they were back at the Ring. Martins said, "You had better go home alone. I'll keep away from you awhile till things have sorted out."

"But nobody can suspect you."

"They are asking about the foreigner who called on Koch yesterday. There may be some unpleasantness for a while."

"Why don't you go to the police?"

"They are so stupid. I don't trust them. See what they've pinned on Harry. And then I tried to hit this man Callaghan. They'll have it in for me. The least they'll do is send me away from Vienna. But if I stay quiet—there's only one person who can give me away. Cooler."

"And he won't want to."

"Not if he's guilty. But then I can't believe he's guilty."

Before she left him, she said, "Be careful. Koch knew so very little and they murdered him. You know as much as Koch."

The warning stayed in his brain all the way to Sacher's: after nine o'clock the streets are very empty, and he would turn his head at every padding step coming up the street behind him, as though that third man whom they had protected so ruthlessly were following him like an executioner. The Russian sentry outside the Grand Hotel looked rigid with the cold, but he was human, he had a face, an honest peasant face with Mongol eyes. The third man had no face: only the top of a head seen from a window. At Sacher's Mr. Schmidt said, "Colonel Calloway has been in, asking after you, sir. I think you'll find him in the bar."

"Back in a moment," Martins said and walked straight out of the hotel again: he wanted time to think. But immediately he stepped outside a man came forward, touched his cap, and said firmly, "Please, sir." He flung open the door of a khaki-painted truck with a Union Jack on the windscreen and firmly urged Martins within. He surrendered without protest; sooner or later, he felt sure, inquiries would be made; he had only pretended optimism to Anna Schmidt.

The driver drove too fast for safety on the frozen road, and Martins protested. All he got in reply was a sullen grunt and a muttered sentence containing the word "orders." "Gave you orders to kill me?" Martins said and got no reply at all. He caught sight of the Titans on the Hofburg balancing great globes of snow above their heads, and then they plunged into ill-lit streets beyond where he lost all sense of direction.

"Is it far?" But the driver paid him no attention at all. At least, Martins thought, I am not under arrest: they have not sent a guard; I am being invited—wasn't that the word they used?—to visit the station to make a statement.

The car drew up and the driver led the way up two flights of stairs; he rang the bell of a great double door, and Martins was aware of many voices beyond it. He turned sharply to the driver and said, "Where the hell . . . ?" but the driver was already halfway down the stairs, and already the door was opening. His eyes were dazzled from the darkness by the lights inside; he heard but he could hardly see the advance of Crabbin. "Oh, Mr. Dexter, we have been so anxious, but better late than never. Let me introduce you to Miss Wilbraham and the Gräfin von Meyersdorf."

A buffet laden with coffee cups; an urn steamed; a woman's face shiny with exertion; two young men with the happy intelligent faces of sixth formers; and, huddled in the background, like faces in a family album, a multitude of the old-fashioned, the dingy, the earnest and cheery features of constant readers. Martins looked behind him, but the door had closed.

He said desperately to Mr. Crabbin, "I'm sorry, but—"

"Don't think any more about it," Mr. Crabbin said. "One cup of coffee and then let's go on to the discussion. We have a very good gathering tonight. They'll put you on your mettle, Mr. Dexter." One of the young men placed a cup in his hand, the other shovelled in sugar before he could say he preferred his coffee unsweetened. The youngest man breathed into his ear, "Afterwards would you mind signing one of your books,

Mr. Dexter?" A large woman in black silk bore down upon him and said, "I don't mind if the Gräfin does hear me, Mr. Dexter, but I don't like your books, I don't approve of them. I think a novel should tell a good story."

"So do I," Martins said hopelessly.

"Now, Mrs. Bannock, wait for question time."

"I know I'm downright, but I'm sure Mr. Dexter values *honest* criticism."

An old lady, whom he supposed was the Gräfin, said, "I do not read many English books, Mr. Dexter, but I am told that yours . . ."

"Do you mind drinking up?" Crabbin said and hustled him through into an inner room where a number of elderly people were sitting on a semicircle of chairs with an air of sad patience.

Martins was not able to tell me very much about the meeting; his mind was still dazed with the death; when he looked up he expected to see at any moment the child Hansel and hear that persistent informative refrain, "Papa, Papa." Apparently Crabbin opened the proceedings, and knowing Crabbin, I am sure that it was a very lucid, very fair and unbiased picture of the contemporary English novel. I have heard him give that talk so often, varied only by the emphasis given to the work of the particular English visitor. He would have touched lightly on various problems of technique—the point of view, the passage of time—and then he would have declared the meeting open for questions and discussions.

Martins missed the first question altogether, but luckily Crabbin filled the gap and answered it satisfactorily. A woman wearing a brown hat and a piece of fur round her throat said with passionate interest,

"May I ask Mr. Dexter if he is engaged on a new work?"

"Oh, yes—yes."

"May I ask the title?"

" 'The Third Man,' " Martins said and gained a spurious confidence as the result of taking that hurdle.

"Mr. Dexter, could you tell us what author has chiefly influenced you?"

Martins, without thinking, said, "Grey." He meant of course the author of *Riders of the Purple Sage,* and he was pleased to find his reply gave general satisfaction —to all save an elderly Austrian who asked, "Grey. What Grey? I do not know the name."

Martins felt he was safe now and said, "Zane Grey —I don't know any other," and was mystified at the low subservient laughter from the English colony.

Crabbin interposed quickly for the sake of the Austrians. "That is a little joke of Mr. Dexter's. He meant the poet Gray—a gentle, mild, subtle genius—one can see the affinity."

"And he is called Zane Grey?"

"That was Mr. Dexter's joke. Zane Grey wrote what we call Westerns—cheap popular novelettes about bandits and cowboys."

"He is not a great writer?"

"No, no. Far from it," Mr. Crabbin said. "In the strict sense I would not call him a writer at all." Martins told me that he felt the first stirrings of revolt at that statement. He had never regarded himself before as a writer, but Crabbin's self-confidence irritated him —even the way the light flashed back from Crabbin's spectacles seemed an added cause of vexation. Crabbin said, "He was just a popular entertainer."

"Why the hell not?" Martins said fiercely.

"Oh, well, I merely meant—"

"What was Shakespeare?"

Somebody with great daring said, "A poet."

"Have you ever read Zane Grey?"

"No, I can't say——"

"Then you don't know what you are talking about."

One of the young men tried to come to Crabbin's rescue. "And James Joyce, where would you put James Joyce, Mr. Dexter?"

"What do you mean put? I don't want to put anybody anywhere," Martins said. It had been a very full day: he had drunk too much with Cooler; he had fallen in love; a man had been murdered—and now he had the quite unjust feeling that he was being got at. Zane Grey was one of his heroes: he was damned if he was going to stand any nonsense.

"I mean would you put him among the really great?"

"If you want to know, I've never heard of him. What did he write?"

He didn't realize it, but he was making an enormous impression. Only a great writer could have taken so arrogant, so original a line. Several people wrote Zane Grey's name on the backs of envelopes and the Gräfin whispered hoarsely to Crabbin, "How do you spell Zane?"

"To tell you the truth, I'm not quite sure."

A number of names were simultaneously flung at Martins—little sharp pointed names like Stein, round pebbles like Woolf. A young Austrian with an ardent intellectual black forelock called out, "Daphne du Maurier," and Mr. Crabbin winced and looked sideways at Martins. He said in an undertone, "Be kind to them."

A gentle kind-faced woman in a hand-knitted jumper said wistfully, "Don't you agree, Mr. Dexter, that no one, no one has written about *feelings* so poetically as Virginia Woolf? In prose, I mean."

Crabbin whispered, "You might say something about the stream of consciousness."

"Stream of what?"

A note of despair came into Crabbin's voice. "Please, Mr. Dexter, these people are your genuine admirers. They want to hear your views. If you knew how they have besieged the Society."

An elderly Austrian said, "Is there any writer in England today of the stature of the late John Galsworthy?"

There was an outburst of angry twittering in which the names of Du Maurier, Priestley, and somebody called Layman were flung to and fro. Martins sat gloomily back and saw again the snow, the stretcher, the desperate face of Frau Koch. He thought: if I had never returned, if I had never asked questions, would that little man still be alive? How had he benefited Harry by supplying another victim—a victim to assuage the fear of whom—Herr Kurtz, Cooler (he could not believe that), Dr. Winkler? Not one of them seemed adequate to the drab gruesome crime in the basement; he could hear the child saying, "I saw the blood on the coke," and somebody turned towards him a blank face without features, a grey plasticine egg, the third man.

Martins could not have said how he got through the rest of the discussion: perhaps Crabbin took the brunt; perhaps he was helped by some of the audience who got into an animated discussion about the film version of a popular American novel. He remembered very little more before Crabbin was making a final speech in his honour. Then one of the young men led him to a table stacked with books and asked him to sign them. "We have only allowed each member one book."

"What have I got to do?"

"Just a signature. That's all they expect. This is my copy of *The Curved Prow*. I would be so grateful if you'd just write a little something . . ."

Martins took his pen and wrote: "From B. Dexter, author of *The Lone Rider of Santa Fe*," and the young man read the sentence and blotted it with a puzzled expression. As Martins sat down and started signing Benjamin Dexter's title pages, he could see in a mirror the young man showing the inscription to Crabbin. Crabbin smiled weakly and stroked his chin, up and down, up and down. "B. Dexter, B. Dexter, B. Dexter." Martins wrote rapidly—it was not, after all, a lie. One by one the books were collected by their owners; little half-sentences of delight and compliment were dropped like curtsies—was this what it was to be a writer? Martins began to feel distinct irritation towards Benjamin Dexter. The complacent, tiring, pompous ass, he thought, signing the twenty-seventh copy of *The Curved Prow*. Every time he looked up and took another book he saw Crabbin's worried speculative gaze. The members of the Institute were beginning to go home with their spoils: the room was emptying. Suddenly in the mirror Martins saw a military policeman. He seemed to be having an argument with one of Crabbin's young henchmen. Martins thought he caught the sound of his own name. It was then he lost his nerve and with it any relic of common sense. There was only one book left to sign; he dashed off a last "B. Dexter" and made for the door. The young man, Crabbin, and the policeman stood together at the entrance.

"And this gentleman?" the policeman asked.

"It's Mr. Benjamin Dexter," the young man said.

"Lavatory. Is there a lavatory?" Martins said.

"I understood a Mr. Rollo Martins came here in one of your cars."

"A mistake. An obvious mistake."

"Second door on the left," the young man said.

Martins grabbed his coat from the cloakroom as he went and made down the stairs. On the first-floor landing he heard someone mounting the stairs and, looking over, saw Paine, whom I had sent to identify him. He opened a door at random and shut it behind him. He could hear Paine going by. The room where he stood was in darkness; a curious moaning sound made him turn and face whatever room it was.

He could see nothing and the sound had stopped. He made a tiny movement and once more it started, like an impeded breath. He remained still and the sound died away. Outside somebody called, "Mr. Dexter, Mr. Dexter." Then a new sound started. It was like somebody whispering—a long continuous monologue in the darkness. Martins said, "Is anybody there?" and the sound stopped again. He could stand no more of it. He took out his lighter. Footsteps went by and down the stairs. He scraped and scraped at the little wheel and no light came. Somebody shifted in the dark, and something rattled in mid-air like a chain. He asked once more with the anger of fear, "Is anybody there?" and only the click-click of metal answered him.

Martins felt desperately for a light switch, first to his right hand and then to his left. He did not dare go farther because he could no longer locate his fellow occupant; the whisper, the moaning, the click had all stopped. Then he was afraid that he had lost the door and felt wildly for the knob. He was far less afraid of the police than he was of the darkness, and he had no idea of the noise he was making.

Paine heard it from the bottom of the stairs and came back. He switched on the landing light, and the glow under the door gave Martins his direction. He opened the door and, smiling weakly at Paine, turned back to take a second look at the room. The eyes of a parrot chained to a perch stared beadily back at him. Paine said respectfully, "We were looking for you, sir. Colonel Calloway wants a word with you."

"I lost my way," Martins said.

"Yes, sir. We thought that was what had happened."

Ten

I had kept a very careful record of Martins' movements from the moment I knew that he had not caught the plane home. He had been seen with Kurtz, and at the Josefstadt Theatre; I knew about his visit to Dr. Winkler and to Cooler, his first return to the block where Harry had lived. For some reason my man lost him between Cooler's and Anna Schmidt's flats; he reported that Martins had wandered widely, and the impression we both got was that he had deliberately thrown off his shadower. I tried to pick him up at the hotel and just missed him.

Events had taken a disquieting turn, and it seemed to me that the time had come for another interview. He had a lot to explain.

I put a good wide desk between us and gave him a cigarette. I found him sullen but ready to talk, within strict limits. I asked him about Kurtz and he seemed to me to answer satisfactorily. I then asked him about Anna Schmidt and I gathered from his reply that he must have been with her after visiting Cooler; that filled in one of the missing points. I tried him with Dr. Winkler, and he answered readily enough. "You've been getting around," I said, "quite a bit. And have you found out anything about your friend?"

"Oh yes," he said. "It was under your nose but you didn't see it."

"What?"

"That he was murdered." That took me by surprise: I had at one time played with the idea of suicide, but I had ruled even that out.

"Go on," I said. He tried to eliminate from his story all mention of Koch, talking about an informant who had seen the accident. This made his story rather confusing, and I couldn't grasp at first why he attached so much importance to the third man.

"He didn't turn up at the inquest, and the others lied to keep him out."

"Nor did your man turn up—I don't see much importance in that. If it was a genuine accident, all the evidence needed was there. Why get the other chap in trouble? Perhaps his wife thought he was out of town; perhaps he was an official absent without leave—people sometimes take unauthorized trips to Vienna from places like Klagenfurt. The delights of the great city, for what they are worth."

"There was more to it than that. The little chap who told me about—they've murdered him. You see they obviously didn't know what else he had seen."

"Now we have it," I said. "You mean Koch."

"Yes."

"As far as we know you were the last person to see him alive." I questioned him then, as I've written, to find out if he had been followed to Koch's by somebody who was sharper than my man and had kept out of sight. I said, "The Austrian police are anxious to pin this on you. Frau Koch told them how disturbed her husband was by your visit. Who else knew about it?"

"I told Cooler." He said excitedly, "Suppose immediately I left he telephoned the story to someone— to the third man. They had to stop Koch's mouth."

"When you told Cooler about Koch, the man was already dead. That night he got out of bed, hearing someone, and went downstairs—"

"Well, that rules me out. I was in Sacher's."

"But he went to bed very early. Your visit brought back the migraine. It was soon after nine that he got up. You returned to Sacher's at nine-thirty. Where were you before that?"

He said gloomily, "Wandering round and trying to sort things out."

"Any evidence of your movements?"

"No."

I wanted to frighten him, so there was no point in telling him that he had been followed all the time. I knew that he hadn't cut Koch's throat, but I wasn't sure that he was quite so innocent as he made out. The man who owns the knife is not always the real murderer.

"Can I have a cigarette?"

"Yes."

He said, "How did you know that I went to Koch's? That was why you pulled me here, wasn't it?"

"The Austrian police—"

"They hadn't identified me."

"Immediately you left Cooler's, he telephoned to me."

"Then that lets him out. If he had been concerned, he wouldn't have wanted to tell you my story—to tell Koch's story, I mean."

"He might assume that you were a sensible man and would come to me with your story as soon as you learned of Koch's death. By the way, how did you learn of it?"

He told me promptly and I believed him. It was then I began to believe him altogether. He said, "I still can't believe Cooler's concerned. I'd stake anything on his honesty. He's one of those Americans with a real sense of duty."

"Yes," I said, "he told me about that when he phoned. He apologized for it. He said it was the worst of having been brought up to believe in citizenship. He said it made him feel a prig. To tell you the truth, Cooler irritates me. Of course he doesn't know that I know about his tire deals."

"Is he in a racket, too, then?"

"Not a very serious one. I daresay he's salted away twenty-five thousand dollars. But I'm not a good citizen. Let the Americans look after their own people."

"I'm damned." He said thoughtfully, "Is that the kind of thing Harry was up to?"

"No. It was not so harmless."

He said, "You know this business—Koch's death—has shaken me. Perhaps Harry did get mixed up in something pretty bad. Perhaps he was trying to clear out again, and that's why they murdered him."

"Or perhaps," I said, "they wanted a bigger cut off the spoils. Thieves fall out."

He took it this time without any anger at all. He said, "We won't agree about motives, but I think you check your facts pretty well. I'm sorry about the other day."

"That's all right." There are times when one has to make a flash decision—this was one of them. I owed him something in return for the information he had given me. I said, "I'll show you enough of the facts in

Lime's case for you to understand. But don't fly off the handle. It's going to be a shock."

It couldn't help being a shock. The war and the peace (if you can call it peace) let loose a great number of rackets, but none more vile than this one. The black marketeers in food did at least supply articles in short supply at extravagant prices. But the penicillin racket was a different affair altogether. Penicillin in Austria was supplied only to the military hospitals: no civilian doctor, not even a civilian hospital, could obtain it by legal means. As the racket started, it was relatively harmless. Penicillin would be stolen and sold to Austrian doctors for very high sums—a phial would fetch anything up to seventy pounds. You might say that this was a form of distribution—unfair distribution because it benefited only the rich patient, but the original distribution could hardly have a claim to greater fairness.

This racket went on quite happily for a while. Occasionally someone was caught and punished, but the danger simply raised the price of penicillin. Then the racket began to get organized: the big men saw big money in it, and while the original thief got less for his spoils, he received instead a certain security. If anything happened to him he would be looked after. Human nature too has curious twisted reasons that the heart certainly knows nothing of. It eased the conscience of many small men to feel that they were working for an employer: they were almost as respectable soon in their own eyes as wage-earners; they were one of a group, and if there was guilt, the leaders bore the guilt. A racket works very like a totalitarian party.

This I have sometimes called stage two. Stage three was when the organizers decided that the profits were not large enough. Penicillin would not always be impossible to obtain legitimately; they wanted more money and quicker money while the going was good. They began to dilute the penicillin with coloured water, and, in the case of penicillin dust, with sand. I keep a small museum in one drawer in my desk, and I showed Martins examples. He wasn't enjoying the talk, but he hadn't yet grasped the point. He said, "I suppose that makes the stuff useless."

I said, "We wouldn't worry so much if that was all, but just consider. You can be immunized from the effects of penicillin. At the best you can say that the use of this stuff makes a penicillin treatment for the particular patient ineffective in the future. That isn't so funny, of course, if you are suffering from V.D. Then the use of sand on a wound that requires penicillin—well, it's not healthy. Men have lost their legs and arms that way—and their lives. But perhaps what horrified me most was visiting the children's hospital here. They had bought some of this penicillin for use against meningitis. A number of children simply died, and a number went off their heads. You can see them now in the mental ward."

He sat on the other side of the desk, scowling into his hands. I said, "It doesn't bear thinking about very closely, does it?"

"You haven't showed me any evidence yet that Harry—"

"We are coming to that now," I said. "Just sit still and listen." I opened Lime's file and began to read. At the beginning the evidence was purely circumstantial, and Martins fidgeted. So much consisted of coincidence—reports of agents that Lime had been at a certain place at a certain time; the accumulation of opportunities; his acquaintance with certain people. He protested once,

"But the same evidence would apply against me—now."

"Just wait," I said. For some reason Harry Lime had grown careless: he may have realized that we suspected him and got rattled. He held a quite distinguished position, and a man like that is the more easily rattled. We put one of our agents as an orderly in the British Military Hospital: we knew by this time the name of our go-between, but we had never succeeded in getting the line right back to the source. Anyway, I am not going to bother the reader now, as I bothered Martins then, with all the stages—the long tussle to win the confidence of the go-between, a man called Harbin. At last we had the screws on Harbin, and we twisted them until he squealed. This kind of police work is very similar to secret service work: you look for a double agent whom you can really control, and Harbin was the man for us. But even he only led us as far as Kurtz.

"Kurtz!" Martins exclaimed. "But why haven't you pulled him in?"

"Zero hour is almost here," I said.

Kurtz was a great step forward, for Kurtz was in direct communication with Lime—he had a small outside job in connection with relief work. With Kurtz, Lime sometimes put things on paper—if he was pressed. I showed Martins the photostat of a note. "Can you identify that?"

"It's Harry's hand." He read it through. "I don't see anything wrong."

"No, but now read this note from Harbin to Kurtz—which we dictated. Look at the date. This is the result."

He read them both through twice.

"You see what I mean?" If one watched a world

come to an end, a plane dive from its course, I don't suppose one would chatter, and a world for Martins had certainly come to an end, a world of easy friendship, hero-worship, confidence that had begun twenty years before—in a school corridor. Every memory—afternoons in the long grass, the illegitimate shoots on Brickworth Common, the dreams, the walks, every shared experience was simultaneously tainted, like the soil of an atomized town. One could not walk there with safety for a long while. While he sat there, looking at his hands and saying nothing, I fetched a precious bottle of whisky out of a cupboard and poured out two large doubles. "Go on," I said, "drink that," and he obeyed me as though I were his doctor. I poured him out another.

He said slowly, "Are you certain that he was the real boss?"

"It's as far back as we have got so far."

"You see he was always apt to jump before he looked."

I didn't contradict him, though that wasn't the impression he had before given of Lime. He was searching round for some comfort.

"Suppose," he said, "someone had got a line on him, forced him into this racket, as you forced Harbin to double cross . . ."

"It's possible."

"And they murdered him in case he talked when he was arrested."

"It's not impossible."

"I'm glad they did," he said. "I wouldn't have liked to hear Harry squeal." He made a curious little dusting movement with his hand on his knee as much as to say, "That's that." He said, "I'll be getting back to England."

"I'd rather you didn't just yet. The Austrian police would make an issue if you tried to leave Vienna at the moment. You see, Cooler's sense of duty made him call them up too."

"I see," he said hopelessly.

"When we've found the third man . . ." I said.

"I'd like to hear him squeal," he said. "The bastard. The bloody bastard."

Eleven

After he left me, Martins went straight off to drink himself silly. He chose the Oriental to do it in, the dreary smoky little night club that stands behind a sham Eastern façade. The same semi-nude photographs on the stairs, the same half-drunk Americans at the bar, the same bad wine and extraordinary gins— he might have been in any third-rate night haunt in any other shabby capital of a shabby Europe. At one point of the hopeless early hours the International Patrol took a look at the scene. Martins had drink after drink; he would probably have had a woman too, but the cabaret performers had all gone home, and there were practically no women left in the place, except for one beautiful shrewd-looking French journalist who made one remark to her companion and fell contemptuously asleep.

Martins moved on: at Maxim's a few couples were dancing rather gloomily, and at a place called Chez Victor the heating had failed and people sat in overcoats drinking cocktails. By this time the spots were swimming in front of Martins' eyes, and he was oppressed by a sense of loneliness. His mind reverted to the girl in Dublin, and the one in Amsterdam. That was one thing that didn't fool you—the straight drink, the simple physical act: one didn't expect fidelity from a woman. His mind revolved in circles—from sentiment to lust and back again from belief to cynicism.

The trams had stopped, and he set out obstinately on foot to find Harry's girl. He wanted to make love to her—just like that: no nonsense, no sentiment. He was in the mood for violence, and the snowy road heaved like a lake and set his mind on a new course towards sorrow, eternal love, renunciation.

It must have been about three in the morning when he climbed the stairs to Anna's room. He was nearly sober by that time and had only one idea in his head, that she must know about Harry too. He felt that somehow this knowledge would pay the mortmain that memory levies on human beings, and he would stand a chance with Harry's girl. If one is in love oneself, it never occurs to one that the girl doesn't know: one believes one has told it plainly in a tone of voice, the touch of a hand. When Anna opened the door to him, with astonishment at the sight of him tousled on the threshold, he never imagined that she was opening the door to a stranger.

He said, "Anna, I've found out everything."

"Come in," she said, "you don't want to wake the house." She was in a dressing gown; the divan had become a bed, the kind of tumbled bed that showed how sleepless the occupant had been.

"Now," she said, while he stood there, fumbling for words, "what is it? I thought you were going to keep away. Are the police after you?"

"No."

"You didn't really kill that man, did you?"

"Of course not."

"You're drunk, aren't you?"

90

"I am a bit," he said sulkily. The meeting seemed to be going on the wrong lines. He said angrily, "I'm sorry."

"Why? I could do with a bit of drink myself."

He said, "I've been with the British police. They are satisfied I didn't do it. But I've learned everything from them. Harry was in a racket—a bad racket." He said hopelessly, "He was no good at all. We were both wrong."

"You'd better tell me," Anna said. She sat down on the bed and he told her, swaying slightly beside the table where her typescript part still lay open at the first page. I imagine he told it to her pretty confusedly, dwelling chiefly on what had stuck most in his mind, the children dead with meningitis and the children in the mental ward. He stopped and they were silent. She said, "Is that all?"

"Yes."

"You were sober when they told you? They really proved it?"

"Yes." He added drearily, "So that, you see, was Harry."

"I'm glad he's dead now," she said. "I wouldn't have wanted him to rot for years in prison."

"But can you understand how Harry—your Harry, my Harry—could have got mixed up . . . ?" He said hopelessly, "I feel as though he had never really existed, that we'd dreamed him. Was he laughing at fools like us all the time?"

"He may have been. What does it matter?" she said. "Sit down. Don't worry." He had pictured himself comforting *her*—not this other way about. She said, "If he was alive now, he might be able to explain, but we've got to remember him as he was to us. There are always so many things one doesn't know about a person, even a person one loves—good things, bad things. We have to leave plenty of room for them."

"Those children—"

She said angrily, "For God's sake stop making people in *your* image. Harry was real. He wasn't just your hero and my lover. He was Harry. He was in a racket. He did bad things. What about it? He was the man we knew."

He said, "Don't talk such bloody wisdom. Don't you see that I love you?"

She looked at him in astonishment. "You?"

"Yes, me. I don't kill people with fake drugs. I'm not a hypocrite who persuades people that I'm the greatest—I'm just a bad writer who drinks too much and falls in love with girls . . ."

She said, "But I don't even know what colour your eyes are. If you'd rung me up just now and asked me whether you were dark or fair or wore a moustache, I wouldn't have known."

"Can't you get him out of your mind?"

"No."

He said, "As soon as they've cleared up this Koch murder, I'm leaving Vienna. I can't feel interested any longer in whether Kurtz killed Harry—or the third man. Whoever killed him it was a kind of justice. Maybe I'd kill him myself under these circumstances. But you still love him. You love a cheat, a murderer."

"I loved a man," she said. "I told you—a man doesn't alter because you find out more about him. He's still the same man."

"I hate the way you talk. I've got a splitting headache, and you talk and talk . . ."

"I didn't ask you to come."

"You make me cross."

Suddenly she laughed. She said, "You are so comic.

You come here at three in the morning—a stranger—and say you love me. Then you get angry and pick a quarrel. What do you expect me to do—or say?"

"I haven't seen you laugh before. Do it again. I like it."

"There isn't enough for two laughs," she said.

He took her by the shoulders and shook her gently. He said, "I'd make comic faces all day long. I'd stand on my head and grin at you between my legs. I'd learn a lot of jokes from the books on after-dinner speaking."

"Come away from the window. There are no curtains."

"There's nobody to see." But automatically checking his statement, he wasn't quite so sure: a long shadow that had moved, perhaps with the movement of clouds over the moon, was motionless again. He said, "You still love Harry, don't you?"

"Yes."

"Perhaps I do. I don't know." He dropped his hands and said, "I'll be pushing off."

He walked rapidly away. He didn't bother to see whether he was being followed, to check up on the shadow. But, passing by the end of the street, he happened to turn and there just around the corner, pressed against a wall to escape notice, was a thick stocky figure. Martins stopped and stared. There was something familiar about that figure. Perhaps, he thought, I have grown unconsciously used to him during these last twenty-four hours; perhaps he is one of those who have so assiduously checked my movements. Martins stood there, twenty yards away, staring at the silent motionless figure in the dark side street who stared back at him. A police spy, perhaps, or an agent of those other men, those men who had corrupted Harry first and then killed him—even possibly the third man?

It was not the face that was familiar, for he could not make out so much as the angle of the jaw; nor a movement, for the body was so still that he began to believe that the whole thing was an illusion caused by shadow. He called sharply, "Do you want anything?" and there was no reply. He called again with the irascibility of drink, "Answer, can't you," and an answer came, for a window curtain was drawn petulantly back by some sleeper he had awakened, and the light fell straight across the narrow street and lit up the features of Harry Lime.

Twelve

"Do you believe in ghosts?" Martins said to me.

"Do you?"

"I do now."

"I also believe that drunk men see things—sometimes rats, sometimes worse."

He hadn't come to me at once with his story—only the danger to Anna Schmidt tossed him back into my office, like something the sea had washed up, tousled, unshaven, haunted by an experience he couldn't understand. He said, "If it had been just the face, I wouldn't have worried. I'd been thinking about Harry, and I might easily have mistaken a stranger. The light was turned off again at once, you see. I only got one glimpse, and the man made off down the street—if he was a man. There was no turning for a long way, but I was so startled I gave him another thirty yards' start. He came to one of those newspaper kiosks and for a moment moved out of sight. I ran after him. It only took me ten seconds to reach the kiosk, and he must have heard me running, but the strange thing was he never appeared again. I reached the kiosk. There wasn't anybody there. The street was empty. He couldn't have reached a doorway without my meeting him. He'd simply vanished."

"A natural thing for ghosts—or illusions."

"But I can't believe I was as drunk as all that!"

"What did you do then?"

"I had to have another drink. My nerves were all to pieces."

"Didn't that bring him back?"

"No, but it sent me back to Anna's."

I think he would have been ashamed to come to me with his absurd story if it had not been for the attempt on Anna Schmidt. My theory when he did tell me his story was that there had been a watcher—though it was drink and hysteria that had pasted on the man's face the features of Harry Lime. That watcher had noted his visit to Anna and the member of the ring—the penicillin ring—had been warned by telephone. Events that night moved fast. You remember that Kurtz lived in the Russian zone—in the second bezirk to be exact, in a wide empty desolate street that runs down to the Prater Platz. A man like that had probably obtained his influential contacts.

The original police agreement in Vienna between the Allies confined the military police (who had to deal with crimes involving Allied personnel) to their particular zones, unless permission was given to them to enter the zone of another power. I had to get on the phone to my opposite number in the American or French zone before I sent in my men to make an arrest or pursue an investigation. Perhaps forty-eight hours would pass before I received permission from the Russians, but in practice there are few occasions when it is necessary to work quicker than that. Even at home it is not always possible to obtain a search warrant or permission from one's superiors to detain a suspect with any greater speed.

This meant that if I wanted to pick up Kurtz it would be as well to catch him in the British zone.

When Rollo Martins went drunkenly back at four o'clock in the morning to tell Anna that he had seen the ghost of Harry, he was told by a frightened porter who had not yet gone back to sleep that she had been taken away by the International Patrol.

What happened was this. Russia, you remember, was in the chair as far as the Innere Stadt was concerned, and the Russians had information that Anna Schmidt was one of their nationals living with false papers. On this occasion, halfway through the patrol, the Russian policeman directed the car to the street where Anna Schmidt lived.

Outside Anna Schmidt's block the American took a hand in the game and demanded in German what it was all about. The Frenchman leaned against the bonnet and lit a stinking Caporal. France wasn't concerned, and anything that didn't concern France had no genuine importance to him. The Russian dug out a few words of German and flourished some papers. As far as they could tell, a Russian national wanted by the Russian police was living there without proper papers. They went upstairs and found Anna in bed, though I don't suppose, after Martins' visit, that she was asleep.

There is a lot of comedy in these situations if you are not directly concerned. You need a background of general European terror, of a father who belonged to a losing side, of house searches and disappearances before the fear outweighs the comedy. The Russian you see, refused to leave the room; the American wouldn't leave a girl unprotected, and the Frenchman—well, I think the Frenchman must have thought it was fun. Can't you imagine the scene? The Russian was just doing his duty and watched the girl all the time, without a flicker of sexual interest; the American stood with his back chivalrously turned; the Frenchman smoked his cigarette and watched with detached amusement the reflection of the girl dressing in the mirror of the wardrobe; and the Englishman stood in the passage wondering what to do next.

I don't want you to think the English policeman came too badly out of the affair. In the passage, undistracted by chivalry, he had time to think, and his thoughts led him to the telephone in the next flat. He got straight through to me at my flat and woke me out of that deepest middle sleep. That was why when Martins rang up an hour later I already knew what was exciting him; it gave him an undeserved but very useful belief in my efficiency. I never had another crack from him about policemen or sheriffs after that night.

When the M.P. went back to Anna's room a dispute was raging. Anna had told the American that she had Austrian papers (which was true) and that they were quite in order (which was rather stretching the truth). The American told the Russian in bad German that they had no right to arrest an Austrian citizen. He asked Anna for her papers and when she produced them, the Russian took them.

"Hungarian," he said, pointing at Anna. "Hungarian," and then, flourishing the papers, "bad, bad."

The American, whose name was O'Brien, said, "Give the goil back her papers," which the Russian naturally didn't understand. The American put his hand on his gun, and Corporal Starling said gently, "Let it go, Pat."

"If those papers ain't in order we got a right to look."

"Just let it go. We'll see the papers at HQ."

"The trouble about you British is you never know when to make a stand."

"Oh, well," Starling said; he had been at Dunkirk, but he knew when to be quiet.

The driver put on his brakes suddenly: there was a road block. You see, I knew they would have to pass this military post. I put my head in at the window and said to the Russian, haltingly, in his own tongue, "What are you doing in the British zone?"

He grumbled that it was "orders."

"Whose orders? Let me see them." I noted the signature—it was useful information. I said, "This tells you to pick up a certain Hungarian national and war criminal who is living with faulty papers in the British zone. Let me see the papers."

He started on a long explanation. I said, "These papers look to me quite in order, but I'll investigate them and send a report of the result to your colonel. He can, of course, ask for the extradition of this lady at any time. All we want is proof of her criminal activities."

I said to Anna, "Get out of the car." I put a packet of cigarettes in the Russian's hand, said, "Have a good smoke," waved my hand to the others, gave a sigh of relief, and that incident was closed.

Thirteen

While Martins told me how he went back to Anna's and found her gone, I did some hard thinking. I wasn't satisfied with the ghost story or the idea that the man with Harry Lime's features had been a drunken illusion. I took out two maps of Vienna and compared them. I rang up my assistant and, keeping Martins silent with a glass of whisky, asked him if he had located Harbin yet. He said no; he understood he'd left Klagenfurt a week ago to visit his family in the adjoining zone. One always wants to do everything oneself; one has to guard against blaming one's juniors. I am convinced that I would never have let Harbin out of our clutches, but then I would probably have made all kinds of mistakes that my junior would have avoided. "All right," I said. "Go on trying to get hold of him."

"I'm sorry, sir."

"Forget it. It's just one of those things."

His young enthusiastic voice—if only one could still feel that enthusiasm for a routine job; how many opportunities, flashes of insight one misses simply because a job has become just a job—his voice tingled up the wire. "You know, sir, I can't help feeling that we ruled out the possibility of murder too easily. There are one or two points—"

"Put them on paper, Carter."

"Yes, sir. I think, sir, if you don't mind my saying so" (Carter is a very young man) "we ought to have him dug up. There's no real evidence that he died just when the others said."

"I agree, Carter. Get on to the authorities."

Martins was right! I had made a complete fool of myself, but remember that police work in an occupied city is not like police work at home. Everything is unfamiliar: the methods of one's foreign colleagues, the rules of evidence, even the procedure at inquests. I suppose I had got into the state of mind when one trusts too much to one's personal judgment. I had been immensely relieved by Lime's death. I was satisfied with the accident.

I said to Martins, "Did you look inside the newspaper kiosk or was it locked?"

"Oh, it wasn't exactly a newspaper kiosk," he said. "It was one of those solid iron kiosks you see everywhere plastered with posters."

"You'd better show me the place."

"But is Anna all right?"

"The police are watching the flat. They won't try anything else yet."

I didn't want to make a fuss and stir in the neighbourhood with a police car, so we took trams—several trams—changing here and there, and came into the district on foot. I didn't wear my uniform, and I doubted anyway, after the failure of the attempt on Anna, whether they would risk a watcher. "This is the turning," Martins said and led me down a side street. We stopped at the kiosk. "You see he passed behind here and simply vanished—into the ground."

"That was exactly where he did vanish to," I said.

"How do you mean?"

An ordinary passer-by would never have noticed that the kiosk had a door, and of course it had been dark when the man disappeared. I pulled the door open and showed to Martins the little curling iron staircase that disappeared into the ground. He said, "Good God, then I didn't imagine him."

"It's one of the entrances to the main sewer."

"And anyone can go down?"

"Anyone."

"How far can one go?"

"Right across Vienna. People used them in air raids; some of our prisoners hid for two years down there. Deserters have used them—and burglars. If you know your way about you can emerge again almost anywhere in the city through a manhole or a kiosk like this one. The Austrians have to have special police for patrolling these sewers." I closed the door of the kiosk again. I said, "So that's how your friend Harry disappeared."

"You really believe it was Harry?"

"The evidence points that way."

"Then whom did they bury?"

"I don't know yet, but we soon shall, because we are digging him up again. I've got a shrewd idea, though, that Koch wasn't the only inconvenient man they murdered."

Martins said, "It's a bit of a shock."

"Yes."

"What are you going to do about it?"

"I don't know. You can bet he's hiding out now in another zone. We have no line now on Kurtz, for Harbin's blown—he must have been blown or they wouldn't have staged that mock death and funeral."

"But it's odd, isn't it, that Koch didn't recognize the dead man's face from the window."

"The window was a long way up and I expect the face had been damaged before they took the body out of the car."

He said thoughtfully, "I wish I could speak to him. You see, there's so much I simply can't believe."

"Perhaps you are the only one who could speak to him. It's risky though, because you do know too much."

"I still can't believe—I only saw the face for a moment." He said, "What shall I do?"

"He won't leave his zone now. The only person who could persuade him to come over would be you—or her, if he still believes you are his friend. But first you've got to speak to him. I can't see the line."

"I could go and see Kurtz. I have the address."

I said, "Remember. Lime may not want you to leave the Russian zone when once you are there, and I can't protect you there."

"I want to clear the whole damned thing up," Martins said, "but I'm not going to act as a decoy. I'll talk to him. That's all."

Fourteen

Sunday had laid its false peace over Vienna; the wind had dropped and no snow had fallen for twenty-four hours. All the morning trams had been full, going out to Grinzing where the young wine was drunk and to the slopes of snow on the hills outside. Walking over the canal by the make-shift military bridge, Martins was aware of the emptiness of the afternoon: the young were out with their toboggans and their skis, and all around him was the after-dinner sleep of age. A notice board told him that he was entering the Russian zone, but there were no signs of occupation. You saw more Russian soldiers in the Inner City than here.

Deliberately he had given Kurtz no warning of his visit. Better to find him out than a reception prepared for him. He was careful to carry with him all his papers, including the laissez-passer of the four powers that on the face of it allowed him to move freely through all the zones of Vienna. It was extraordinarily quiet over here on the other side of the canal, and a melodramatic journalist had painted a picture of silent terror; but the truth was simply the wide streets, the greater shell damage, the fewer people—and Sunday afternoon. There was nothing to fear, but all the same, in this huge empty street where all the time you heard your own feet moving, it was difficult not to look behind.

He had no difficulty in finding Kurtz's block, and when he rang the bell the door was opened quickly, as though Kurtz expected a visitor, by Kurtz himself.

"Oh," Kurtz said, "it's you, Rollo," and made a perplexed motion with his hand to the back of his head. Martins had been wondering why he looked so different, and now he knew. Kurtz was not wearing the toupee, and yet his head was not bald. He had a perfectly normal head of hair cut close. He said, "It would have been better to have telephoned to me. You nearly missed me; I was going out."

"May I come in a moment?"

"Of course."

In the hall a cupboard door stood open, and Martins saw Kurtz's overcoat, his raincoat, a couple of soft hats, and, hanging sedately on a peg like a wrap, Kurtz's toupee. He said, "I'm glad to see your hair has grown," and was astonished to see, in the mirror on the cupboard door, the hatred flame and blush on Kurtz's face. When he turned Kurtz smiled at him like a conspirator and said vaguely, "It keeps the head warm."

"Whose head?" Martins asked, for it had suddenly occurred to him how useful that toupee might have been on the day of the accident. "Never mind," he went quickly on, for his errand was not with Kurtz. "I'm here to see Harry."

"Harry?"

"I want to talk to him."

"Are you mad?"

"I'm in a hurry, so let's assume that I am. Just make a note of my madness. If you should see Harry—or his ghost—let him know that I want to talk to him. A ghost isn't afraid of a man, is it? Surely it's the other way round. I'll be waiting in the Prater by the Big Wheel for the next two hours—if you can get in touch with the dead, hurry." He added, "Remember, I was Harry's friend."

Kurtz said nothing, but somewhere, in a room off the hall, somebody cleared his throat. Martins threw open a door: he had half expected to see the dead rise yet again, but it was only Dr. Winkler who rose from a kitchen stove, and bowed very stiffly and correctly with the same celluloid squeak.

"Dr. Winkle," Martins said. Dr. Winkler looked extraordinarily out of place in a kitchen. The debris of a snack lunch littered the kitchen table, and the unwashed dishes consorted very ill with Dr. Winkler's cleanness.

"Winkler," the doctor corrected him with stony patience.

Martins said to Kurtz, "Tell the doctor about my madness. He might be able to make a diagnosis. And remember the place—by the Great Wheel. Or do ghosts only rise by night?" He left the flat.

For an hour he waited, walking up and down to keep warm, inside the enclosure of the Great Wheel; the smashed Prater with its bones sticking crudely through the snow was nearly empty. One stall sold thin flat cakes like cartwheels, and the children queued with their coupons. A few courting couples would be packed together in a single car of the Wheel and revolve slowly above the city, surrounded by empty cars. As the car reached the highest point of the Wheel, the revolutions would stop for a couple of minutes and far overhead the tiny faces would press against the glass. Martins wondered who would come for him. Was there

enough friendship left in Harry for him to come alone,
or would a squad of police arrive? It was obvious from
the raid on Anna Schmidt's flat that he had a certain
pull. And then as his watch hand passed the hour, he
wondered: was it all an invention of my mind? are
they digging up Harry's body now in the Central Cemetery?

Somewhere behind the cake stall a man was whistling, and Martins knew the tune. He turned and waited.
Was it fear or excitement that made his heart beat—
or just the memories that tune ushered in, for life
had always quickened when Harry came, came just
as he came now, as though nothing much had happened, nobody had been lowered into a grave or found
with cut throat in a basement, came with his amused
deprecating take-it-or-leave-it manner—and of course
always took it.

"Harry."

"Hullo, Rollo."

Don't picture Harry Lime as a smooth scoundrel.
He wasn't that. The picture I have of him on my files
is an excellent one: he is caught by a street photo-
grapher with his stocky legs apart, big shoulders a little
hunched, a belly that has known too much good food
too long, on his face a look of cheerful rascality, a
geniality, a recognition that his happiness will make
the world's day. Now he didn't make the mistake of
putting out a hand that might have been rejected, but
instead just patted Martins on the elbow and said,
"How are things?"

"We've got to talk, Harry."

"Of course."

"Alone."

"We couldn't be more alone than here."

He had always known the ropes, and even in the

107

smashed pleasure park he knew them, tipping the woman in charge of the Wheel, so that they might have a car to themselves. He said, "Lovers used to do this in the old days, but they haven't the money to spare, poor devils, now," and he looked out of the window of the swaying, rising car at the figures diminishing below with what looked like genuine commiseration.

Very slowly on one side of them the city sank; very slowly on the other great cross girders of the Wheel rose into sight. As the horizon slid away the Danube became visible, and the piers of the Reichsbrücke lifted above the houses. "Well," Harry said, "it's good to see you, Rollo."

"I was at your funeral."

"That was pretty smart of me, wasn't it?"

"Not so smart for your girl. She was there too— in tears."

"She's a good little thing," Harry said. "I'm very fond of her."

"I didn't believe the police when they told me about you."

Harry said, "I wouldn't have asked you to come if I'd known what was going to happen, but I didn't think the police were on to me."

"Were you going to cut me in on the spoils?"

"I've never kept you out of anything, old man, yet."

He stood with his back to the door as the car swung upwards, and smiled back at Rollo Martins, who could remember him in just such an attitude in a secluded corner of the school quad, saying, "I've learned a way to get out at night. It's absolutely safe. You are the only one I'm letting in on it." For the first time Rollo Martins looked back through the years without admiration, as he thought, He's never grown up. Marlowe's devils wore squibs attached to their tails: evil was like Peter Pan—it carried with it the horrifying and horrible gift of eternal youth.

Martins said, "Have you ever visited the children's hospital? Have you see any of your victims?"

Harry took a look at the toy landscape below and came away from the door. "I never feel quite safe in these things," he said. He felt the back of the door with his hand, as though he were afraid that it might fly open and launch him into the iron-ribbed space. "Victims?" he asked. "Don't be melodramatic, Rollo. Look down there," he went on, pointing through the window at the people moving like black flies at the base of the Wheel. "Would you really feel any pity if one of those dots stopped moving—forever? If I said you can have twenty thousand pounds for every dot that stops, would you really, old man, tell me to keep my money—without hesitation? Or would you calculate how many dots you could afford to spare? Free of income tax, old man. Free of income tax." He gave his boyish conspiratorial smile. "It's the only way to save nowadays."

"Couldn't you have stuck to tires?"

"Like Cooler? No, I've always been ambitious.

"But they can't catch me, Rollo, you'll see. I'll pop up again. You can't keep a good man down." The car swung to a standstill at the highest point of the curve and Harry turned his back and gazed out of the window. Martins thought: one good shove and I could break the glass, and he pictured the body dropping among the flies. He said, "You know the police are planning to dig up your body. What will they find?"

"Harbin," Harry replied with simplicity. He turned away from the window and said, "Look at the sky."

The car had reached the top of the Wheel and hung there motionless, while the stain of the sunset ran in streaks over the wrinkled papery sky beyond the black girders.

"Why did the Russians try to take Anna Schmidt?"

"She had false papers, old man."

"I thought perhaps you were just trying to get her here—because she was your girl? Because you wanted her?"

Harry smiled. "I haven't all that influence."

"What would have happened to her?"

"Nothing very serious. She'd have been sent back to Hungary. There's nothing against her really. She'd be infinitely better off in her own country than being pushed around by the British police."

"She hasn't told them anything about you."

"She's a good little thing," Harry repeated with complacent pride.

"She loves you."

"Well, I gave her a good time while it lasted."

"And I love her."

"That's fine, old man. Be kind to her. She's worth it. I'm glad." He gave the impression of having arranged everything to everybody's satisfaction. "And you can help to keep her mouth shut. Not that she knows anything that matters."

"I'd like to knock you through the window."

"But you won't, old man. Our quarrels never last long. You remember that fearful one in the Monaco, when we swore we were through. I'd trust you anywhere, Rollo. Kurtz tried to persuade me not to come but I know you. Then he tried to persuade me to, well, arrange an accident. He told me it would be quite easy in this car."

"Except that I'm the stronger man."

"But I've got the gun. You don't think a bullet wound would show when you hit *that* ground?" Again the car began to move, sailing slowly down, until the flies were midgets, were recognizable human beings. "What fools we are, Rollo, talking like this, as if I'd do that to you—or you to me." He turned his back and leaned his face against the glass. One thrust . . . "How much do you earn a year with your Westerns, old man?"

"A thousand."

"Taxed. I earn thirty thousand free. It's the fashion. In these days, old man, nobody thinks in terms of human beings. Governments don't, so why should we? They talk of the people and the proletariat, and I talk of the mugs. It's the same thing. They have their five-year plans and so have I."

"You used to be a Catholic."

"Oh, I still *believe,* old man. In God and mercy and all that. I'm not hurting anybody's soul by what I do. The dead are happier dead. They don't miss much here, poor devils," he added with that odd touch of genuine pity, as the car reached the platform and the faces of the doomed-to-be-victims, the tired pleasure-hoping Sunday faces, peered in at them. "I could cut you in, you know. It would be useful. I have no one left in the Inner City."

"Except Cooler? And Winkler?"

"You really mustn't turn policeman, old man." They passed out of the car and he put his hand again on Martins' elbow. "That was a joke, I know you won't. Have you heard anything of old Bracer recently?"

"I had a card at Christmas."

"Those were the days, old man. Those were the days. I've got to leave you here. We'll see each other— sometime. If you are in a jam, you can always get me at Kurtz's." He moved away and, turning, waved the hand he had had the tact not to offer: it was like the whole past moving off under a cloud. Martins suddenly called after him, "Don't trust me, Harry," but there was too great a distance now between them for the words to carry.

Fifteen

"Anna was at the theatre," Martins told me, "for the Sunday matinée. I had to see the whole thing through a second time. About a middle-aged pianist and an infatuated girl and an understanding—a terribly understanding—wife. Anna acted very badly—she wasn't much of an actress at the best of times. I saw her afterwards in her dressing room, but she was badly fussed. I think she thought I was going to make a serious pass at her all the time, and she didn't want a pass. I told her Harry was alive—I thought she'd be glad and that I would hate to see how glad she was, but she sat in front of her make-up mirror and let the tears streak the grease paint and I wished after that she had been glad. She looked awful and I loved her. Then I told her about my interview with Harry, but she wasn't really paying much attention because when I'd finished she said, "I wish he was dead."

"He deserves to be."

"I mean he would be safe then—from everybody."

I asked Martins, "Did you show her the photographs I gave you—of the children?"

"Yes. I thought, it's got to be kill or cure this time. She's got to get Harry out of her system. I propped the

113

pictures up among the pots of grease. She couldn't avoid seeing them. I said, 'The police can't arrest Harry unless they get him into this zone, and we've got to help!'

"She said, 'I thought he was your friend.' I said, 'He *was* my friend.' She said, 'I'll never help you to get Harry. I don't want to see him again, I don't want to hear his voice. I don't want to be touched by him, but I won't do a thing to harm him.'

"I felt bitter—I don't know why, because after all I had done nothing for her. Even Harry had done more for her than I had. I said, 'You want him still,' as though I were accusing her of a crime. She said, 'I don't want him, but he's in me. That's a fact—not like friendship. Why, when I have a love dream, he's always the man.' "

I prodded Martins on when he hesitated. "Yes?"

"Oh, I just got up and left her then. Now it's your turn to work on me. What do you want me to do?"

"I want to act quickly. You see it was Harbin's body in the coffin, so we can pick up Winkler and Cooler right away. Kurtz is out of our reach for the time being, and so is the driver. We'll put in a formal request to the Russians for permission to arrest Kurtz and Lime: it makes our files tidy. If we are going to use you as our decoy, your message must go to Lime straight away—not after you've hung around in this zone for twenty-four hours. As I see it you were brought here for a grilling almost as soon as you got back into the Inner City; you heard then from me about Harbin; you put two and two together and you go and warn Cooler. We'll let Cooler slip for the sake of the bigger game—we have no evidence he was in on the penicillin racket. He'll escape into the second bezirk to Kurtz, and Lime will know you've played the game. Three hours later you send a message that the police are after you: you are in hiding and must see him."

"He won't come."

"I'm not so sure. We'll choose our hiding place carefully—where he'll think there's a minimum of risk. It's worth trying. It would appeal to his pride and his sense of humour if he could scoop you out. And it would stop your mouth."

Martins said, "He never used to scoop me out—at school." It was obvious that he had been reviewing the past with care and coming to conclusions.

"That wasn't such serious trouble and there was no danger of your squealing."

He said, "I told Harry not to trust me, but he didn't hear."

"Do you agree?"

He had given me back the photographs of the children and they lay on my desk. I could see him take a long look at them. "Yes," he said, "I agree."

Sixteen

All the first arrangements went according to plan. We delayed arresting Winkler, who had returned from the second bezirk, until after Cooler had been warned. Martins enjoyed his short interview with Cooler. Cooler greeted him with patronage. "Why, Mr. Martins, it's good to see you. Sit down. I'm glad everything went off all right between you and Colonel Calloway. A very straight chap, Calloway."

"It didn't," Martins said.

"You don't bear any ill will, I'm sure, about my letting him know about you seeing Koch. The way I figured it was this—if you were innocent you'd clear yourself right away and if you were guilty, well, the fact that I liked you oughtn't to stand in the way. A citizen has his duties."

"Like giving false evidence at an inquest."

Cooler said, "Oh, that old story. I'm afraid you are riled at me, Mr. Martins. Look at it this way—you as a citizen, owing allegiance—"

"The police have dug up the body. They'll be after you and Winkler. I want you to warn Harry . . ."

"I don't understand."

"Oh, yes, you do." And it was obvious that he did.

116

Martins left him abruptly. He wanted no more of that kindly tired humanitarian face.

It only remained then to bait the trap. After studying the map of the sewer system I came to the conclusion that a café anywhere near the main entrance of the great sewer, which was placed in what Martins had mistakenly called a newspaper kiosk—would be the most likely spot to tempt Lime. He had only to rise once again through the ground, walk fifty yards, bring Martins back with him, and sink again into the obscurity of the sewers. He had no idea that this method of evasion was known to us: he probably knew that one patrol of the sewer police ended before midnight, and the next did not start till two, and so at midnight Martins sat in the little cold café in sight of the kiosk, drinking coffee after coffee. I had lent him a revolver; I had men posted as close to the kiosk as I could, and the sewer police were ready when zero hour struck to close the manholes and start sweeping the sewers inwards from the edge of the city. But I intended if I could to catch him before he went underground again. It would save trouble—and risk to Martins. So there, as I say, in the café Martins sat.

The wind had risen again, but it had brought no snow; it came icily off the Danube and in the little grassy square by the café it whipped up the snow like the surf on top of a wave. There was no heating in the café, and Martins sat warming each hand in turn on a cup of ersatz coffee—innumerable cups. There was usually one of my men in the café with him, but I changed them every twenty minutes or so irregularly. More than an hour passed. Martins had long given up hope and so had I, where I waited at the end of a phone several streets away, with a party of the sewer police ready to go down if it became necessary.

We were luckier than Martins because we were warm in our great boots up to the thighs and our reefer jackets. One man had a small searchlight about half as big again as a car headlight strapped to his breast, and another man carried a brace of Roman candles. The telephone rang. It was Martins. He said, "I'm perishing with cold. It's a quarter past one. Is there any point in going on with this?"

"You shouldn't telephone. You must stay in sight."

"I've drunk seven cups of this filthy coffee. My stomach won't stand much more."

"He can't delay much longer if he's coming. He won't want to run into the two o'clock patrol. Stick it another quarter of an hour, but keep away from the telephone."

Martins' voice said suddenly, "Christ, he's here. He's—" and then the telephone went dead. I said to my assistant, "Give the signal to guard all manholes," and to my sewer police, "We are going down."

What had happened was this. Martins was still on the telephone to me when Harry Lime came into the café. I don't know what he heard, if he heard anything. The mere sight of a man wanted by the police and without friends in Vienna speaking on the telephone would have been enough to warn him. He was out of the café again before Martins had put down the receiver. It was one of those rare moments when none of my men was in the café. One had just left and another was on the pavement about to come in. Harry Lime brushed by him and made for the kiosk. Martins came out of the café and saw my men. If he had called out then it would have been an easy shot, but it was not, I suppose, Lime the penicillin racketeer who was escaping down the street; it was Harry. He hesitated just long enough for Lime to put the kiosk between them then he called out, "That's him," but Lime had already gone to ground.

What a strange world unknown to most of us lies under our feet: we live above a cavernous land of waterfalls and rushing rivers, where tides ebb and flow as in the world above. If you have ever read the adventures of Allan Quartermain and the account of his voyage along the underground river to the city of Molosis, you will be able to picture the scene of Lime's last stand. The main sewer, half as wide as the Thames, rushes by under a huge arch, fed by tributary streams: these streams have fallen in waterfalls from higher levels and have been purified in their fall, so that only in these side channels is the air foul. The main stream smells sweet and fresh with a faint tang of ozone, and everywhere in the darkness is the sound of falling and rushing water. It was just past high tide when Martins and the policeman reached the river: first the curving iron staircase, then a short passage so low they had to stoop, and then the shallow edge of the water lapped at their feet. My man shone his torch along the edge of the current and said, "He's gone that way," for just as a deep stream when it shallows at the rim leaves an accumulation of debris, so the sewer left in the quiet water against the wall a scum of orange peel, old cigarette cartons, and the like, and in this scum Lime had left his trail as unmistakably as if he had walked in mud. My policeman shone his torch ahead with his left hand, and carried his gun in his right. He said to Martins, "Keep behind me, sir, the bastard may shoot."

"Then why the hell should you be in front?"

"It's my job, sir." The water came halfway up their legs as they walked; the policeman kept his torch pointing down and ahead at the disturbed trail at the sewer's edge. He said, "The silly thing is the bastard doesn't stand a chance. The manholes are all guarded and we've cordoned off the way into the Russian zone. All our chaps have to do now is to sweep inwards down the side passes from the manholes." He took a whistle out of his pocket and blew, and very far away here and again there came the notes of the reply. He said, "They are all down here now. The sewer police, I mean. They know this place just as I know the Tottenham Court Road. I wish my old woman could see me now," he said, lifting his torch for a moment to shine it ahead, and at that moment the shot came. The torch flew out of his hand and fell in the stream. He said, "God blast the bastard."

"Are you hurt?"

"Scraped my hand, that's all. Here, take this other torch, sir, while I tie my hand up. Don't shine it. He's in one of the side passages." For a long time the sound of the shot went on reverberating: when the last echo died a whistle blew ahead of them, and Martins' companion blew an answer.

Martins said, "It's an odd thing—I don't even know your name."

"Bates, sir." He gave a low laugh in the darkness. "This isn't my usual beat. Do you know the Horseshoe, sir?"

"Yes."

"And the Duke of Grafton?"

"Yes."

"Well, it takes a lot to make a world."

Martins said, "Let me come in front. I don't think he'll shoot at me, and I want to talk to him."

"I had orders to look after you, sir, careful."

"That's all right." He edged round Bates, plunging a foot deeper in the stream as he went. When he was in front he called out, "Harry," and the name set up

120

an echo, "Harry, Harry, Harry!" that travelled down the stream and woke a whole chorus of whistles in the darkness. He called again, "Harry. Come out. It's no use."

A voice startling close made them hug the wall. "Is that you, old man?" it called. "What do you want me to do?"

"Come out. And put your hands above your head."

"I haven't a torch, old man. I can't see a thing."

"Be careful, sir," Bates said.

"Get flat against the wall. He won't shoot at me," Martins said. He called, "Harry, I'm going to shine the torch. Play fair and come out. You haven't got a chance." He flashed the torch on, and twenty feet away, at the edge of the light and the water, Harry stepped into view. "Hands above the head, Harry." Harry raised his hand and fired. The shot ricocheted against the wall a foot from Martins' head, and he heard Bates cry out. At the same moment a searchlight from fifty yards away lit the whole channel, caught Harry in its beams, Martins, the staring eyes of Bates slumped at the water's edge with the sewage washing to his waist. An empty cigarette carton wedged into his armpit and stayed. My party had reached the scene.

Martins stood dithering there above Bates's body, with Harry Lime halfway between us. We couldn't shoot for fear of hitting Martins, and the light of the searchlight dazzled Lime. We moved slowly on, our revolvers trained for a chance, and Lime turned this way and that way like a rabbit dazzled by headlights; then suddenly he took a flying jump into the deep central rushing stream. When we turned the searchlight after him he was submerged, and the current of the sewer carried him rapidly on, past the body of Bates, out of the range of the searchlight into the dark. What makes a man, without hope, cling to a few more minutes of existence? Is it a good quality or a bad one? I have no idea.

Martins stood at the outer edge of the searchlight beam, staring downstream. He had his gun in his hand now, and he was the only one of us who could fire with safety. I thought I saw a movement and called out to him, "There. There. Shoot." He lifted his gun and fired, just as he had fired at the same command all those years ago on Brickworth Common, fired, as he did then, inaccurately. A cry of pain came tearing back like calico down the cavern: a reproach, an entreaty. "Well done," I called and halted by Bates's body. He was dead. His eyes remained blankly open as we turned the searchlight on him; somebody stooped and dislodged the carton and threw it in the river, which whirled it on—a scrap of yellow Gold Flake: he was certainly a long way from the Tottenham Court Road.

I looked up and Martins was out of sight in the darkness. I called his name and it was lost in a confusion of echoes, in the rush and the roar of the underground river. Then I heard a third shot.

Martins told me later, "I walked down stream to find Harry, but I must have missed him in the dark. I was afraid to lift the torch: I didn't want to tempt him to shoot again. He must have been struck by my bullet just at the entrance of a side passage. Then I suppose he crawled up the passage to the foot of the iron stairs. Thirty feet above his head was the manhole, but he wouldn't have had the strength to lift it, and even if he had succeeded the police were waiting above. He must have known all that, but he was in great pain, and just as an animal creeps into the dark to die, so I suppose a man makes for the light. He wants to die at home, and the darkness is never home to *us*. He began to pull himself up the stairs, but then the pain took him and he couldn't go on. What made him whistle that absurd scrap of a tune I'd been fool enough to believe he had written himself? Was he trying to attract attention, did he want a friend with him, even the friend who had trapped him, or was he delirious and had he no purpose at all? Anyway I heard his whistle and came back along the edge of the stream, and felt the wall end and found my way up the passage where he lay. I said, 'Harry," and the whistling stopped, just above my head. I put my hand on an iron handrail and climbed. I was still afraid he might shoot. Then, only three steps up, my foot stamped down on his hand, and he was there. I shone my torch on him: he hadn't got a gun; he must have dropped it when my bullet hit him. For a moment I thought he was dead, but then he whimpered with pain. I said, 'Harry,' and he swivelled his eyes with a great effort to my face. He was trying to speak, and I bent down to listen. 'Bloody fool,' he said—that was all. I don't know whether he meant that for himself—some sort of act of contrition, however inadequate (he was a Catholic)—or was it for me—with my thousand a year taxed and my imaginary cattle rustlers who couldn't even shoot a rabbit clean? Then he began to whimper again. I couldn't bear it any more and I put a bullet through him."

"We'll forget that bit," I said.

Martins said, "I never shall."

Seventeen

A thaw set in that night, and all over Vienna the snow melted, and the ugly ruins came to light again: steel rods hanging like stalactites, and rusty girders thrusting like bones through the grey slush. Burials were much simpler than they had been a week before when electric drills had been needed to break the frozen ground. It was almost as warm as a spring day when Harry Lime had his second funeral. I was glad to get him under earth again, but it had taken two men's deaths. The group by the grave was smaller now: Kurtz wasn't there, nor Winkler—only the girl and Rollo Martins and myself. And there weren't any tears.

After it was over the girl walked away without a word to either of us down the long avenue of trees that led to the main entrance and the tram stop, splashing through the melted snow. I said to Martins, "I've got transport. Can I give you a lift?"

"No," he said, "I'll take a tram back."

"You win, you've proved me a bloody fool."

"I haven't won," he said. "I've lost." I watched him striding off on his overgrown legs after the girl. He caught her up and they walked side by side. I don't think he said a word to her: it was like the end of a story. He was a very bad shot and a very bad judge of character, but he had a way with Westerns (a trick of tension) and with girls (I wouldn't know what). And Crabbin? Oh, Crabbin is still arguing with the British Cultural Relations Society about Dexter's expenses. They say they can't pass simultaneous payments in Stockholm and Vienna. Poor Crabbin. Poor all of us when you come to think of it.

About the Author

Graham Greene was born in 1904 and educated at Berkhamsted School, where his father was the headmaster. On coming down from Balliol College, Oxford, where he published a book of verse, he worked for four years as a sub-editor on *The Times*. He established his reputation with his fourth novel, *Stamboul Train,* which he classed as an "entertainment" in order to distinguish it from more serious work. In 1935 he made a journey across Liberia, described in *Journey Without Maps,* and on his return was appointed film critic of the *Spectator*. In 1926 he had been received into the Roman Catholic Church and was commissioned to visit Mexico in 1938 and report on the religious persecution there. As a result he wrote *The Lawless Roads* and, later, *The Power and the Glory*.

Brighton Rock was published in 1938, and in 1940 he became literary editor of the *Spectator*. The next year he undertook work for the Foreign Office and was sent out to Sierra Leone in 1941–43. One of his major postwar novels, *The Heart of the Matter,* is set in West Africa and is considered by many to be his finest book. This was followed by *The End of the Affair, The Quiet American,* a story set in Vietnam, *Our Man in Havana,* and *A Burnt-Out Case*. His most recent novels are *The Comedians, Travels with My Aunt,* and *The Honorary Consul*. In 1967 he published a collection of short stories under the title: *May We Borrow Your Husband?* His autobiography, *A Sort of Life,* was published in 1971.

In all, Graham Greene has written some thirty novels, "entertainments," plays, children's books, travel books, and collections of essays and short stories. He was made a Companion of Honour in 1966.